ONLY THE PERFECT

ONLY YOU, BOOK 2

ELLE THORPE

WWW.ELLETHORPE.COM

For Kirsty, for always asking where the next chapter is. xxx

JAMISON

*T*he midnight blue Toyota Starlet pulled up at the curb with a screech of tyres, the body of the vehicle rocking backwards as if it hadn't expected the abrupt halt. I ducked my head to peer through the window to the young guy behind the wheel. He waved me in. I hesitated for a moment, wondering what the odds were of escaping this drive without a case of whiplash, before I lifted the handle and slid into the seat next to him. The Uber driver's dreadlocked hair brushed his shoulders as he held his fist out for me to bump. I obliged with a smile. If he liked me enough, maybe he wouldn't get me killed.

"Ridgemont Hotel, right? On Sussex Street?"

"Thanks, mate."

He nodded and turned his attention to the road, while I turned mine to my phone. "Hey, sorry. I'm back. What were you saying?"

"You were about to tell me why you're going to this wedding again. Because I still don't understand." Disbelief tinted Low's tone, despite the fact we'd already had this conversation once.

I cradled the phone between my chin and shoulder as I

dragged my seatbelt across my suit jacket. "Because I was invited?"

"But why you agreed to go is still a mystery. Bree is a nasty piece of work for even inviting you. You know she just wants to shove her rich new husband in your face. You dodged a bullet with that one, Jam."

The driver made a sharp turn onto a side street and my shoulder bumped against the window. I eyed him warily, hoping he knew where he was going. And that we'd make it there in one piece. The reception started in a few minutes.

"I know you never liked her, but she wasn't all bad."

Low scoffed.

"Okay. She was pretty bad. But we can't all be as lucky as you. You already have the love of your life. Maybe mine is one of her bridesmaids." I grinned as we pulled up outside the hotel.

"Bree will *love* that."

I laughed. "I know, right?"

"You're evil."

"Just a starving student who's looking forward to a meal that isn't two-minute noodles." I unclicked my seatbelt, mouthed *thank you* at my driver, and gave him a wave before getting out and closing the door. "Gotta go, Low. I'm here."

"Well, have fun. Would it be wrong of me to hope the groom trips on Bree's dress and falls on his cheating face?"

I shook my head, unable to wipe the grin from my face. Hanging up without bothering to say goodbye, because we never did, I tucked my phone into the pocket of my suit pants and took the steps to the entranceway two at a time. A sign announcing the wedding of Mr. and Mrs. Christoperson pointed me in the direction of the ballroom, and I whistled as I strolled across the hotel foyer. I was oddly excited to be attending the wedding of my ex-girlfriend. I didn't think she'd expected me to say yes. But why not? I liked weddings. Free food, free booze, a bit of dancing—what's not to like?

I checked the sign by the ballroom door, finding my name under table number thirty-three. Thirty-three? Bloody hell. I knew Rick the Dick was rich, but that number of tables at a wedding seemed excessive. As if they had that many friends. I'd only met Rick once when they'd come into the bar where I worked, presumably so Bree could flaunt the man she'd cheated on me with. It had been one too many times. He'd snapped his fingers at me like I was his manservant and stuck his pointy nose in the air as he looked over the racecourse. Sure, it had been late in the afternoon, and a lot of the racegoers were getting sloppy drunk, but something told me Rick wouldn't have approved anyway. He probably preferred polo or lacrosse or some other sport that made him feel superior to us commoners. Not much ruffled my feathers, but their overdone loved-up shit had gotten tiresome quickly. I'd been relieved when Bree had given up fawning all over him and gone home.

Pulling open the ballroom door, I paused as the noise cut out and a roomful of eyes turned in my direction. Shit. I guess being on time didn't cut it at this wedding. The MC glanced over at me, before choosing to ignore my presence, and continued on with his announcements. My eyes met Bree's across the room and she glared. I winked, just to piss her off, and made my way through the sea of tables to the back of the room where I eventually found table thirty-three.

Back of the room was an understatement. Table thirty-three was so far away from the bridal table it was almost in another fancily dressed postcode. Suited me just fine. Except, as I looked for a gap, all the seats were taken. I frowned, wondering if I'd read the seating chart wrong.

"Sorry, is this your seat?" a woman on the other side of the table called, pulling a little boy from the chair next to her and settling him on her lap. "He has a chair at another table," she explained, then dropped a kiss on the top of his blond head.

He stuck his bottom lip out and looked up at her with puppy-dog eyes. "But I want to stay with you, Mummy!"

I sidestepped between chairs and made my way to my spot, sitting down on the white covered seat with its garish pink bow tied to the back. So ugly. But Bree always had loved pink.

"Nathan, you can't," the woman said to the little boy. She pointed across the room. "Your dad wants you to sit over there by him tonight. This is a special day for him, remember? And you have a special spot right up at the front."

I glanced over curiously, not wanting to eavesdrop but intrigued none the less. Had she pointed at the bridal table?

"But I don't want to! He's sitting with Bree and I hate Bree. She's mean."

"Nathan!" his mother scolded. "We don't hate anyone!" But the tiniest of smiles pulled at the corner of her lips, and I could see her fighting back her laugh. Her green eyes held a hint of mischief as she struggled to keep a serious face.

I leaned closer to her and whispered, only just loud enough for her to hear, "I kind of hate her too, for the record. He's not wrong about her being mean."

She chuckled, her hand coming up to cover her mouth. But not before I'd caught a glimpse of her smile—wide and full of shining white teeth. Her nose was small and turned up slightly at the end like a pixie. And her light brown hair swept her shoulders in gentle waves. She was pretty. Gentle-looking, in her lacy, kinda sexy dress that showed off just enough creamy-looking skin to captivate my attention.

She put her hands over Nathan's ears. "I'm not a member of her fan club either, but don't encourage him. She's his new step-mother so he will have to learn to like her."

"You're Rick the Dick's ex?" I asked, making sure her hands were still over Nathan's ears.

She choked on a laugh. "That's not what I called him when we were married. Well, not to his face anyway." Nathan wriggled free from his makeshift earmuffs and slid off her lap to chase an older boy out onto the dance floor. From across the room, I watched Bree wrinkle her nose at the children playing and fought back the urge to roll my eyes.

"I'm Elodie Christopers—sorry, Elodie Chalmers. I've gone back to my maiden name, but it's only been a few weeks so I keep forgetting. Old habits die hard." She stuck her hand out for me to shake.

"Jamison. So, they stuck us exes together, huh?"

Her eyebrows pulled together in confusion.

"I'm Bree's ex."

Understanding dawned on her face. "Seriously? It doesn't sound like you think much of the happy couple. Why did you come?"

I wondered if she even realised she'd pulled a face when she'd said the words *happy couple*. Her nose had wrinkled adorably.

"Why does everyone keep asking me that? For the free food, obviously." I picked up a bread roll from the centre of the table and took a bite to accentuate my point.

She laughed, the sound musical, and a sharp contrast to the MC's droning voice. "So, you're on better terms with them then?"

She quirked an eyebrow. "Uh, no. I guess not. Rick only told me he was leaving two months ago, and now he's married."

I whistled long and low. "Bloody hell, are you two even legally divorced?"

She nodded. "He must have paid someone off, because it went through about two weeks ago."

"Wow."

Her gaze darkened as she looked around the room. "I wonder how long they were planning this before he even bothered to break up with me."

I took in the room full of tables, cream and pink flowers on every available surface, fairy lights hanging from the ceiling, and the wedding dress that fit Bree's food-starved body to perfection.

5

She squinted at the five-tier wedding cake. "It doesn't look like they threw this together last minute, does it?"

"Not really." I didn't mention I'd received my invite at least six weeks earlier. And that I'd walked in on Rick and Bree having sex in her apartment well before that.

Elodie sat tall in her seat with her shoulders pulled back. That tiny smile at the corners of her mouth remained, and it fascinated me. I don't think I'd have been half as calm and poised as she was. Bree and I had only been together for six months, and I'd spent a good few weeks moping after I'd caught her cheating before realising that she'd done us both a favour. The pretty woman in the next chair had been married to this guy. Committed. Whether she knew or not that he'd cheated—because he had, the timescales didn't lie—she must be hating this.

"Does all this not bother you?"

Her shoulders slumped as a long sigh escaped her. When she spoke again, her voice sounded more wistful than sad. "Honestly? One ex to another? It bothers me when I think about when we first got together. We were high-school sweethearts. But I don't see that boy in Rick anymore." She looked down and fidgeted with the edge of the tablecloth. "And I'm sad for Nathan. He doesn't understand that Rick moving out has nothing to do with him. I didn't want this for him. I thought I'd done such a good job of finding someone committed and reliable and…"

She looked up and shook her head. "I'm so sorry. I don't know why I'm telling you all of this."

The fear she had for her little boy and his well-being proved to me again that this woman was Bree's polar opposite. Bree didn't give a toss about anyone but herself. Elodie seemed selfless, and I wouldn't hesitate to bet she'd lay her life on the line for that kid. I could see the weight of hers and Rick's decisions weighed heavily on her, so I gave her a grin, trying to lighten the mood. "Hey, I'm just happy to have someone to talk to. We rejects over here at table thirty-three have to stick together, right?"

The creases between her eyebrows smoothed out as she straightened her shoulders. "Right."

The rest of the table all seemed to be over eighty or under seventeen. Plus one middle-aged man that had so far spent the entire time I'd been sitting here buttering a bread roll, wiping the butter off, then buttering it again. "Do you know any of these people?" I asked under my breath. "Bree doesn't have any family, none that I ever met anyway. I don't know anyone here."

"Nope, not one. I was thinking about pulling my Kindle out of my bag before you came along."

I stifled a grin. "No Kindle necessary. We might be at the left-overs table, but we have free booze and a free meal and later on, we'll do some free dancing. Deal?"

She glanced over at the bridal party table where Bree had her tongue shoved down Rick's throat, the MC cheering them on now that the speeches were done. I gagged a little and Elodie scrunched her nose again. "There's only so much of that I can watch sober. You have a deal."

2

ELODIE

I didn't want to go home.

I hadn't exactly been dreading the wedding, but I was annoyed that Rick had railroaded me into going. We had no mutual friends I could talk to, despite being together for eight years. Which should have been a warning sign something was wrong between us. My friends had never liked Rick. And Rick had no friends. Just acquaintances. People he used to move his way up the corporate ladder. His lack of real friendships had never seemed to bother him, if he'd even noticed. His family had always been nice enough when we'd been together, but ever since he'd left me, his family had given me the cold shoulder. As if being married to their son for the past seven years, not to mention the mother of his child, meant nothing. Which was incredibly disappointing. I was doing everything in my power to make this separation amicable, because Nathan deserved parents who could speak civilly to each other. He deserved to have birthday parties with both his parents present. He deserved to get school awards without worrying about whether his parents would run into each other and make a scene in front of his friends. I was managing to put aside my feelings over Rick's unfaithfulness. The fact his family couldn't look at me made me wonder what he'd told them.

I may not have wanted to be there, but I'd had Nathan to look after, so I'd come here with a purpose. But Nathan had ditched me in favour of following his older cousin around all night, leaving me with nothing to do.

Nothing to do but talk to the hottest guy I'd laid eyes on in years.

A little voice in my head cautioned that maybe I was only finding Jamison so attractive because I'd had two glasses of wine and he was the first man to pay any attention to me since high school. Since I'd been married to Rick, I'd changed. Stopped being interesting to people. Even to myself. So, being the centre of someone's attention tonight had been different and exciting.

But it was nine o'clock, and I was about to turn into a pumpkin. I sighed as I noticed my mother wave from the doorway of the ballroom and then make her way over to where I was sitting. I waved back, and Jamison gave a low whistle. "Who's the silver fox?"

I elbowed him in the ribs while I laughed. "Stop. That's my mother." Her hair was magnificent under the low ballroom lighting. She'd stopped dying it years ago and it was now a complete silvery grey I had always thought suited her better than the dark brown she'd once sported. She'd permed it recently and the curls bounced around her cheerful face.

"She's late. She missed dinner."

I snorted, then covered my mouth with my hand, my eyes widening as he chuckled. He'd been making me laugh all night, making fun of Rick and Bree, telling me bad jokes and stories about the bar where he worked. "She's not a guest. She's here to pick me up."

His smile fell. "What? You aren't leaving?"

I nodded. "It's late for Nathan. I need to get him home and into bed."

Truthfully, I'd asked Mum to come pick us up so I would have an excuse to leave. I knew by nine Rick would have had enough of Nathan's presence, and I'd have had more than enough of Rick and Bree. But now, after sitting with Jamison all evening, I regretted asking her to come at all. It shocked me to realise I'd actually been having fun.

Jamison clutched my hand, pulling it to his chest. "You can't leave me alone at table thirty-three!"

Not for the first time, my skin buzzed when he touched me and feelings I hadn't felt in a long time stirred within me. Pleasant, warm sensations that made me crave more. Earlier in the night, he'd passed me a tray of butter and when our fingers had brushed, I'd felt it like a jolt of electricity. We'd inched closer together as we'd talked, since we'd mostly been making fun of the couple and didn't want people to overhear, and every so often, his leg touched mine beneath the table. I'd been surprised at how much I'd focussed on it happening again. And by how many times I'd been the one to make it happen.

I tilted my head and smiled apologetically. I didn't move my hand though, liking the way it felt enclosed between his. "Sorry."

There was a lull in the eighties tune playing and Mum cleared her throat behind me. When I glanced over my shoulder, she smiled.

"Jamison, this is my mother, Barbara. Mum, this is Jamison. He's Bree's ex."

Why did I add that? Mum raised her eyebrow, taking in my hand still clutched within Jamison's. I pulled it back slowly.

"You don't have to come home yet if you're having a good time, sweetheart. I can take Nathan with me."

I paused. *Wasn't that idea appealing. Appealing, but not possible. Ugh.* Regretfully, I shook my head. "I should be there to tuck him in."

"Pfft." Mum waved away my concerns. "It's after nine p.m. and he's been running around all day. He'll be asleep before I even pull out of the hotel driveway. All I'll be doing is carrying him to his bed." She gave me an intentional look, her eyes shifting to Jamison. "Stay, have a good time. You deserve a night off."

I felt a blush heat my cheeks. Just like my friends, Mum had never liked Rick. She'd barely been able to contain her excitement when we'd split. But she could go easy on the apparent matchmaking she was trying to pull here.

Still, I did want to stay. One night off from my life. One night off from trying to be perfect all the time.

I hesitated, but as I took in Jamison's pleading face, I felt my resolve disintegrate. "Don't leave me, El. I can't very well dance with Nanna June over there, can I?" He tilted his head to the old woman who'd drifted off to sleep about half an hour earlier.

El? I'd always hated people shortening my name, but for some reason, it didn't bother me now. I kind of liked the way it sounded on his lips. My eyes dropped to said lips and my tongue ran over my own. I lifted my eyes to Jamison's, just in time to see something in his gaze change. It was so subtle I wasn't sure I actually saw it. But a warmth curled through me anyway.

"Stay," he said again. Emotions warred within me. If I stayed to hang out with Jamison, at some point, Rick would notice. Would he care? Would he flip out or somehow punish me for it later by making my life difficult? We'd been together for years, but I no longer felt like I knew him. As much as I hated it, our lives were forever interconnected, and right now, our relationship was very civil. Despite the way he'd left us, I'd been cool and calm and level-headed. Nathan needed that from me. I'd already failed at giving him parents who loved each other; the very least I could do was to stay on friendly terms with his father.

But the alcohol, watching Rick with Bree, and flirting with Jamison—one or more of those made me want to agree. We hadn't even danced yet, and I'd be lying if I said a huge part of me wasn't wondering what moving in his arms would feel like. Running my hands up his biceps, snaking them around his neck as he pulled me close and whispered in my ear… My toes curled just thinking about being that close to him.

My gaze travelled the room for Nathan and found him sitting on Rick's lap. Nathan's blond hair was sweaty and his eyelids were drooping from exhaustion. Rick smoothed his hair back, then leant in and kissed Bree over the top of his head. Something within me hardened. Why was Rick allowed to move on while I sat at home alone?

I'd turned into a wallflower, I realised with a start. Rick was opinionated about everything, and we'd once spent hours debating over the things we both believed in. But as we'd grown up, those debates had turned into arguments I didn't enjoy, and so I'd avoided them. I'd barely noticed myself fading further and further into his shadow, until suddenly he wasn't there anymore. I didn't like the person I'd become. Sitting here, at Rick's wedding, talking to a hot guy who had to be at least five years younger than I was… It felt good. I felt noticed and like a little of the old me had emerged from the shadows.

"Are you sure?" I met my mother's eyes and she gave me a triumphant smile and a quick kiss on the cheek.

"Positive. Just come get him from my place in the morning."

Jamison gave a triumphant whoop. Mum's gaze slid over to him. "And I trust you'll get my daughter home safe, young man."

"Jesus Christ," I muttered, standing up and tucking my arm beneath my mother's before I tugged her across the room toward Nathan. "She's going now. I'll be back in a minute," I called back to Jamison.

"I'll be waiting."

Why did those words make my stomach flip in anticipation?

Jamison

Somewhere around my third beer I'd started finding Elodie

incredibly attractive. Not that I needed beer to see how pretty she was, but she wasn't my normal type. Elodie was the complete and utter opposite of Bree. She was soft where Bree was hard. She had curves where Bree was so skinny her bones stuck out. She was quiet and gentle, where Bree was loud and obnoxious. And she was real, where Bree was fake. Bree was everything that normally caught my eye, but Elodie sparked my interest in a way my ex never had. I'd started up the conversation to be friendly, but somewhere along the line I'd gone past being friendly into being genuinely interested. I needed to know her better.

She sunk back into her seat, just as the lights dimmed and the MC called the newly married couple onto the floor for their first dance.

She dropped her voice to a whisper as the opening strains of Bree and Rick's wedding song started up. "They're gone."

I raised my eyebrows at her suggestively, unable to hide my grin. Nathan was a bloody cute kid, but knowing I had Elodie all to myself now made me a happy man. She laughed before turning to face the dance floor. I loved that she found me funny. Bree never had.

We both watched as Rick and Bree waltzed awkwardly around the centre of the room. Rick stepped on Bree's dress and she lurched forward, shooting him a dirty look before she remembered her fake smile. I couldn't help the chuckle that escaped me. "It's like a train wreck I can't look away from." I shook my head. "Good luck to the poor bugger."

"Oh, don't feel sorry for him. He's as high maintenance as she is. This is likely all one big show to him. He would have designed all this to impress his business partners and associates. That's the only reason he ever threw a party when we were together anyway."

As the song ended, Rick spun Bree around and dipped her, the split on her dress revealing almost too much as she pointed her foot in the air. I rolled my eyes and Elodie snorted before coughing to cover it, glancing around as if she were worried somebody would think she was laughing at them. I pushed the glass of wine toward her that I'd bought while she was with her mum.

"You were drinking red, right?"

She nodded as she pulled the glass toward her. "I'm not a fan of champagne; it gives me a headache. But the red is good." She took a swallow, her tongue running over her lips, before she placed the glass back on the table.

"Well, drink up. I figure we'll need to be more than slightly buzzed to make it through this spectacle..." I trailed off as Bree and Rick moved to the cake-cutting table. They cut a piece together then Rick picked it up and fed it carefully into Bree's mouth. "I bet she warned him not to ruin her makeup by shoving it into her face."

"Probably. I would have liked to have seen that though—ugh, I know it's their wedding, but do they have to keep doing that?"

"There's so much tongue in that kiss I'm questioning if either of them might have been a giraffe in a past life."

Elodie snorted and took a large gulp of her wine. "We need way more alcohol to deal with this. I haven't had a night away from Nathan in forever, so I'll risk the hangover."

"Cheers then," I toasted, clinking my glass together with hers.

Her eyes met mine. "Cheers to you for making this night fun."

"You ain't seen nothin' yet, kid." I drained the last of my drink and held my hand out to her. The DJ had started up dance music, with LMFAO's "Party Rock Anthem" blaring through the speakers. "It's dancing time, and I do a mean Running Man."

She slapped her hand in mine, grinning as she stood. She was above average height in her heels, but she still seemed tiny from my 6'3" vantage point. She tipped her head back. "Your Running Man ain't got nothin' on my Sprinkler with a twist!"

"With a twist? Well, if I wasn't interested before, I am now." I led her through the crowd, until we were right in the middle of the floor, and broke out my best Running Man moves, pumping my arms and sliding my feet back and forth. Elodie stuck one arm in the air, her other arm bent so she could rest her hand behind her head, and her hips jerked to the beat as she spun back and forth. She only lasted a moment before she doubled over laughing.

"What? That all you got?" I panted out. Who knew a few minutes of Running Man would be so exhausting?

"Your Running Man looks more like the funky chicken!" She burst into a fresh round of laughter and my heart flipped. There was nothing girl next door about her when she laughed like that. Her eyes, bright with amusement, lit up her whole face.

"Oh yeah? What about your Sprinkler!" I imitated her moves, thrilled that she had to wipe her eyes from laughing so hard.

She grabbed my arm and pulled me closer, gasping around her laughs and clutching her stomach. "Stop, before I pee myself. We're already making a scene."

I glanced around, my gaze eventually settling on Bree. She was back at the bridal table shooting me death looks. Whatever. The people next to us had moved back to avoid our flailing limbs, but the only other people watching us were smiling. Everyone else was too busy dancing and having a good time to pay attention to us. The song changed to "Love Shack" by the B-52's and Elodie gasped. "Yes! I love this song!"

Bree sliced the air beneath her chin with flattened fingers, telling me to cut it out. God she was a bitch. She'd invited me here and she'd done nothing but glare at me all night. We were just having fun, yet every time I looked over, Bree was glaring.

"Do you know all the words?" I yelled in Elodie's ear.

She grinned and nodded as her hips swivelled and she danced closer.

"Come on, then." I grabbed her arm and pulled her to the stage next to the little DJ booth where two microphones stood on stands.

Her eyes grew wide. "Wait. What are you doing?"

I shrugged. "Having fun?" I gave the DJ a questioning thumbs up and he laughed, gesturing for me to go ahead. I passed Elodie a mic and she shook her head.

"Jesus Christ."

I winked at her before flicking the microphone on and belting out the next line of the song.

ELODIE

Jamison was not only delicious to look at, but he could sing too. Shame about his dancing skills. Still, I grinned at him as he sang out the chorus of "Love Shack." He strutted around the tiny stage like he owned it, people on the dance floor crowding him and singing along. He even held the mic out for Rick's aunty to sing a line like a full-fledged rock star. He was owning this impromptu karaoke while I stood, slightly terrified, at the back of the stage.

My eyes met Rick's across the room. He was sitting next to Bree at the bridal table. She had a face like thunder and looked ready to kill Jamison, while Rick's eyes bored into mine. I knew that look. I'd seen it time and time again over the years. It was a cold, creeping expression that said "Shut up, Elodie. You're embarrassing yourself." I dropped my gaze to the floor. But then Jamison's shoes appeared in my line of vision and his fingers tipped my chin up as he said into the microphone, "Don't be shy now, Elodie. Your fans are waiting to hear you sing."

His enthusiasm was contagious, energy radiating from him like sunshine. And the crowd were feeling it. They cheered, a sea of happy, smiling faces below me. My eyes met Rick's again, as Jamison moved his mic away from his mouth and said in my ear, "Fuck them. Sing with me."

And when I looked back into his hazel eyes, he flicked his

head toward the centre of the stage. A smile spread across my face as I let his sunshine fill me and I lifted the microphone to my mouth and sang the last chorus like I was Madonna performing at Madison Square Garden.

Tomorrow, I'd blame the wine for this. I'd blame it even more for what happened next.

The song finished, and I glanced at Jamison. His grin stretched ear to ear. "That. Was. Epic." His gaze dropped to my lips.

My already racing heart picked up another notch. I stepped toward him feeling confident and free after standing up to Rick, even in such a small, indirect way. "Yeah, it was."

He closed the gap between us, or maybe I did, but his hand grabbed the back of my head as his lips crashed down onto mine. My brain shut down as lust mixed with excitement swirled through me. My hands slid up his chest, and I kissed him back. His tongue moved against my lips and I opened for him, wanting more of the way he felt, and enjoying the sudden heat rising everywhere our bodies touched. Our tongues moved together, and I couldn't remember the last time I'd been kissed like this. Had Rick ever kissed me with this much passion? Jamison kissed as if he was thinking about throwing me down on the bridal table and taking me right here in front of three hundred people. And a large part of me would have been totally down for that.

"What the hell are you two doing?!" Bree's voice shrieked in my ear.

I jerked away from Jamison's mouth and realised the entire room was now watching us, not just Bree, who stood with her arms folded beneath her fake boobs, her chest heaving with her anger. I glanced around, my eyes widening as they met Jamison's. Holy shit. We'd made a really big scene.

A laugh twitched at his lips, and instantly, my rising panic disappeared. My own laugh bubbled in my throat.

"Want to get out of here?" he whispered in my ear.

"Hell yes."

He slid his fingers between mine.

"Well, uh. Thanks for having us, Bree."

"Get out!" she screeched, pointing one long, red talon at the door. Jamison and I both stifled laughs as we stumbled off the stage and ran for the door.

3

JAMISON

"Did we really just get kicked out of the wedding?" I laughed softly against Elodie's lips.

She pulled back, her eyes slightly unfocused and her hair a tousled halo from where I'd been running my fingers through it. Her lips were already swollen from the fast and furious make-out session we'd been having in the back seat of the taxi.

"Bree wasn't a fan of your singing, apparently." She grinned, and I leant in to kiss her again, unable to get enough of her.

"Fuck, you're beautiful," I mumbled against her skin.

City lights flashed by in a blur outside the window as I let my lips trail off the side of her mouth, along her jaw to the spot beneath her ear. I watched in fascination as her head dropped back and her eyes closed. My cock thickened behind the fly of my suit pants. "Come home with me," I whispered.

She moaned quietly as my tongue circled the shell of her ear. "I want to, but I shouldn't."

"Okay." I paused and sat back. "Is this," I motioned between us, "still alright, though?"

Her fingers snaked into my hair, pulling my head to her mouth. Her lips were hot and demanding, sending fire through my veins. Her breasts rubbed against my chest until I wanted to ease her down on the back seat and cover my body with hers—driver be damned.

"I've got to get Nathan in the morning."

My fingers skated over her hip and up her ribcage, my thumb stopping just below the swell of her breast. "Okay."

"We only just met."

I pulled away, my lips hovering just over hers, and smiled gently. "It's fine. Really." I meant it. I'd had an amazing evening with her, and if this was as far as it went, that was more than okay with me. "You'll be worth waiting for."

"We're here," the driver announced with a glance in the rearview mirror. I'd expected him to be leering at us after we'd just spent fifteen minutes going to second base in the back seat of his car. But he looked thoroughly bored, as if he saw this sort of thing every night. Maybe he did.

My lips brushed over Elodie's. "This is me. Are you sure you're okay to go the rest of the way on your own?" I'd wanted the taxi driver to take her home first, but she'd refused, insisting her place was further and that she'd be fine alone. I handed the driver a few notes, making sure to give him more than enough to cover Elodie for the rest of her trip home.

She nodded and glanced over my shoulder at my townhouse. "Yeah, I'll be..." She bit her bottom lip as her eyes locked with mine. My heart thumped, seemingly only to push lust through my veins. I wanted her with every ounce of my being, and despite respecting her boundaries, I was damn disappointed this was ending here. But I could wait as long as she wanted. I was a patient man, even when my cock was so hard I was surprised it hadn't exploded into pieces.

"Oh, screw it." Her lips slammed into mine again and my heart leapt. Did that mean...?

She pushed the door open and we tumbled out, a mess of limbs, neither of us wanting to break the kiss. I slammed the door behind me with my foot and found her hands, lacing my fingers between them as I walked her backwards up the path. "Are you sure?" I asked, breaking away to study her face as we tripped up the front steps. I rummaged through my pockets for the key.

She nodded, but then she bit her lip again. "You should know though…I've never been with anyone other than Rick."

I paused. "No one?"

She shook her head. "High-school sweethearts, remember?"

"Okay," I said slowly. I wanted this, but at the same time, this had to be huge for her. I rested my back on the door. I didn't want to ruin it by rushing. "We don't have to do anything you don't want to. Just because you're coming in, doesn't mean I expect anything. We can just hang out. Watch Netflix…"

"And chill?"

A laugh rumbled through me. "Your call." Opening the door, I led her in, not bothering to flick on the light. I hoped my room-mate Mark was doing nightshift at the club he owned.

She tugged on my hand until I twisted back around. "Jamison?"

"Yes?"

"Chilling is good. I want to chill."

I gathered her into my arms with a wicked grin and dropped a kiss on her upturned face. Then I led her up the stairs.

ELODIE

My libido had taken over my head. What was I doing? Going home with some guy I'd only met a few hours before. This wasn't me. I wasn't an eighteen-year-old, picking men up in bars. Not that I'd ever actually done that, since I'd always had Rick around, but this didn't fit the faithful mother and wife image I'd crafted over the last few years either.

Being a faithful wife wasn't exactly all it was cracked up to be, though, was it? I'd had the perfect husband, but he'd turned out to be not so perfect after all. I was still mourning that loss. But Jamison was sweet and funny and handsome. He'd focused his sole attention on me. And I liked it. My stomach flip-flopped as I followed him up the narrow staircase of his two-story town-house. But the lack of kissing gave me too much time to think.

Did he realise I was older than him? I'd guessed him to be around twenty-two, so I only had a few years on him, but still. I'd had a baby. I wasn't ashamed of the stretch marks beneath my belly button, but would he find me attractive naked? Rick hadn't been overly interested in sex with me for years, which I now attributed to him getting it from other sources, but his lack of interest hadn't been great for my body confidence either. I tried to keep myself fit so I could keep up with Nathan, but there was nothing I could do about the stretch marks. They were just part of who I was.

"Oh good, they're not here," Jamison said, as we passed a dark-ened bedroom. My stomach dropped.

"They?" *Please, Lord, don't let him live with his parents.* I would die a thousand deaths if he'd brought me back to his parent's place.

Jamison stopped in the doorway of the other bedroom across the hall and pulled me into his arms. I welcomed the opportunity to explore the hard planes of his body, letting my hands roam his back and untucking his shirt from his suit pants as I went. His eyes twinkled with mischief, as if he knew exactly what I was thinking. "My roommate and his partner. Mark owns a night-club, so he works weird hours. But it's Saturday, so he probably won't be home until three or four a.m."

Relief loosened the tightness in my muscles. I'd be long gone by three a.m.

"So," Jamison said, "This is my room..." He let go of me to flick on a lamp and I peered into his space. It was tidy. A neatly made double bed sat in the middle of the room with a navy-blue quilt covering it. A *Star Wars* poster hung above it, and a desk in the corner of the room was covered in a pile of law textbooks. It was the only thing in the room that wasn't neatly aligned.

Jamison hovered around the bed looking indecisive, and I wasn't sure what to do next either. I suddenly felt a whole lot more sober than I had in the back of the taxi. I walked over to his desk and trailed my fingers over his books before glancing over at him. "You're a law student?"

He sat down on the edge of the bed as he nodded. "I'm just about done. I took a year off to travel after high school, otherwise I'd be finished by now."

"That's great."

"What about you?"

I shook my head. "I always wanted to go to Uni. I even considered doing law as well. But we got married as soon as we turned eighteen, and then I fell pregnant with Nathan almost right away. I found a job I love though, so it all worked out in the end."

"So, that makes you, what? Twenty-four?"

"Twenty-five."

A smile spread across his face. "Cougar."

I laughed. I liked the way he teased. He hadn't once made me uncomfortable. Everything about him seemed good-natured and jovial. Even when we'd spoken about Bree and Rick, his mocking had never felt malicious. We probably shouldn't have made out in front of them, though. That was bad form, and I'd apologise to Rick next time I saw him. He'd expect it. And he was easier to deal with when he wasn't in a mood.

"You can't be that much younger than me if you've nearly finished your law degree."

He shook his head and patted the bed beside him. I crossed the room and perched on the edge of the mattress. "I'm not. I'm twenty-three."

Older than I'd guessed. That was good. "So, nice room..."

"Thanks."

God. Was sex with a random stranger always this awkward? We'd had no problems talking all evening and we'd been all over each other on the way here, but now I seemed to have nothing interesting to add to the conversation.

Silence. I could literally hear crickets outside the window. Maybe I should just leave? But when did I ever get to do this sort of thing? When did I ever get to be young and a little bit reckless? I was always somebody's wife, somebody's mum, somebody's employee. When did I ever just get to be me? I eyed the door, but when I glanced back at him, our eyes locked.

"I'm sorry, this is weird, isn't it?" he asked with a self-depreciating chuckle.

I let out a breath. "No, it's me. I don't know what I'm doing."

"I don't either. But I really want to kiss you again. Is that okay?"

My insides turned to mush. Rick had never once asked so politely if he could kiss me. I nodded. Jamison inched forward on the bed, leaning his long torso in until his breath warmed my skin. His lips met mine, soft and sweet, sending tingles across my mouth. He cupped one cheek in his large hand, his fingers resting gently just below my ear as he kissed me, until his lips parted and he deepened the kiss. I relaxed into his touch, feeling some of the awkward tension between us evaporate. We kissed soft and slow for a long time before his hands snaked around my back and found the zipper on my dress. My stomach flipped, but this time it was fuelled by excitement, not nerves.

His fingertips brushed my spine as he dragged the zipper down. I tilted my head to the side, tucking my hair behind my ear as he slipped his hand beneath the strap of my dress and pushed it over one shoulder. I shivered as he took his time, kissing every inch of skin. His kisses moved across my shoulder, and he pushed the strap of my bra in the same direction the dress had fallen a moment earlier.

My hands trailed up his chest, pulling at his white collared shirt as I went, untucking it from the front of his pants as I'd done to the back earlier. I opened my eyes to find the buttons on his shirt, and undid them swiftly, pushing aside the material. A lick of delicious heat seared through me as I took in his chest and abs. He wasn't built like a man that spent hours in a gym, but he was long and lean with a dusting of freckles across his tan chest. I leant forward and kissed one experimentally, feeling the hard muscle underneath my lips. He obviously did some sort of exercise regularly, and I drank him in, committing his form to memory for when I'd no doubt want to replay this moment in my head later.

Goosebumps travelled over me as he unhooked the clasp at my back letting my breasts fall free. The room wasn't well lit by the lamp, but it was far from dark. Was he happy with what he saw? I'd only ever been this naked with one other man, and doubts began to crowd my thoughts. But he kissed me again, before taking both breasts in his hands, his thumbs flicking over the nipples. I hissed as pleasure shot straight to my core, and he pushed me gently toward the mattress.

"Jamison…"

His lips skated over my collarbone, trailing feather-light kisses across my skin until I was flat on my back. His tongue circled my nipple and my toes curled as his big body pressed me into the mattress. His tongue flicked over the tip, eliciting a gasp from me, and his palms skated down my sides, pushing my dress down as he went.

"Yes?" he mumbled, finally breaking away from skin long enough to answer. I pushed his shirt off his arms, enjoying the way his biceps flexed as he shifted his weight to drop the shirt on the floor. His mouth immediately returned to my breasts.

"Nothing," I mumbled as he sucked me into his mouth. Jesus

Christ. I could feel wetness pooling between my thighs. Every swipe of his tongue reinforced the gut instinct that told me this would be different. That *he* was different. And that I'd forgotten what it felt like to have a man take his time with me.

Jamison

My cock was so hard I was probably stabbing a hole in Elodie's leg. But fuck. Elodie in her near-naked glory had heat licking straight south. For a few awkward moments I'd thought she'd leave, but as soon as we'd started kissing again, everything had gone back to feeling right. And now I had her writhing beneath me and I'd barely even touched her. Her body became more responsive with every inch of her I explored.

I dragged my tongue down the underside of her breast and placed open-mouthed kisses across the gentle swell of her stomach. She tensed as I reached her belly button, and I lifted my head searching out her eyes. "You still okay?"

She propped herself up on her elbow. Which gave me a great view of her tits. Perky with the nipples shiny and erect from my mouth. My dick throbbed for attention, but I ignored it, more concerned with why she'd suddenly frozen up.

"Yeah, I just...my stomach is all scarred." I looked down. I couldn't see any scars in the dim light, but I ran my fingers over the softness above her underwear and felt the change in the skin.

"Does it hurt?" I asked, frowning.

"No, not at all. They're old. From when I was pregnant with Nathan."

I crawled back up her body, and pressed my lips to hers, pushing her back down on the bed. "Then what's the problem?"

She shrugged and turned her cheek into the pillow.

I dropped my nose to her neck and ran it up to her ear, before whispering, "You're the sexiest woman I've ever had in my bed, Elodie. I don't give a shit about your scars."

That little smile I was beginning to associate with her reappeared and I slid back down her torso, determined to show her exactly how perfect I thought her body was, scars and all. My tongue found the groove of her hip bones and traced a path up and down each and every stretch mark, delighting in the way her muscles bunched and tensed beneath me. Her thighs fell apart slightly, and I took that as a sign she wanted more. I ran my fingers under the elastic of her underwear, teasingly slow, before slipping it down her legs. She lifted her head again to watch as I settled between her thighs. And fuck. I nearly came, just knowing her eyes would be on me as I went down on her.

My tongue darted out to run through her folds and I held back a chuckle as her head dropped back into the pillows. I circled her clit for a long, luxurious moment before I quit messing around and sucked her tiny bud between my lips. Her back arched and her fingers threaded through my hair as a moan escaped her. The gentle pressure on the back of my head urged me on. I added a finger to my attentions on her pussy, sliding it through her wetness then up inside her.

"Ah, just—" She twisted slightly beneath me, her face pained.

"Shit, sorry. Did I hurt you?"

"It's just...a weird angle." Then she giggled. "Not exactly like the movies, huh?"

I moved my fingers slightly, angling my wrist up and her frown smoothed out as she relaxed back into the bed. "More like the movies now?" It probably came out sounding slick, but I honestly wanted to know.

A sigh floated across the space between us as I went back to stroking her with my tongue. I'd take that as an affirmative. I watched the way she moved and listened to the sounds she made, a desperate need to get her off spurring me on. Some primal, caveman-like instinct in me wanted to make her come harder than Rick ever had. Make her forget that Rick even existed. I added another slick finger, and her hips began to move. Following her cues, I pumped my fingers in and out, in time with her movements. The little sounds she was making made my balls ache with the need to get inside her, but nothing was more important in that moment than her.

She groaned, but I didn't let up until her thighs constricted around my head and her walls clenched in on my fingers. Her breath came in pants as her body shuddered, her pussy clenching again, before she went still. Then her head popped up, a smile lighting up her face.

"Uh, thanks?" She laughed.

I grinned as I sat up, my dick throbbing at the sight of her naked, post-orgasm blushed body. That manly pride that always appeared whenever you made your woman come coursed through me. She grasped my zipper and I reached across her, grabbing a condom from the drawer beside my bed.

She tugged, but the zipper caught, and her big green eyes looked up at me. "You're going to have to stand up to get these off."

"Oh, right. Yeah." I leapt up wrenching my fly the rest of the way down and let my suit pants fall to the ground. She wriggled to the side of the bed and pushed my boxer briefs down my legs. Her mouth hovered near the tip of my dick and damn if it wasn't the sexiest she'd looked yet. Her tongue darted out and licked the wetness from the tip before pulling back and taking the condom from my hand. Her fingers stroked me, making my legs tremble before she rolled the latex over my length.

Shifting back up the bed, she looked much more comfortable with her nakedness now that I was on display too. Or maybe she was still feeling the aftereffects of her orgasm. Either way, her actions welcomed me to her, and I went eagerly. Lining up the tip of my cock with her entrance, I found her lips with my own. I pressed my lips to hers, hard and demanding. "You still want to chill?"

She groaned, and I wondered if it was because of my pathetic joke or the fact that my dick was nudging inside of her. It sounded like a little of both, and I didn't know her well enough yet to know one way or the other. But then she pulled me down on top of her, so we were skin on skin and I forgot all about my dumb one-liners. The tip of my cock slipped inside her with the movement, and I braced myself on my forearms to take some of my weight off her. Her hips thrust to meet mine and my cock disappeared into her, nearly overwhelming me with the tight, wet heat of her.

Elodie whispered in my ear, "What do you think?"

4

ELODIE

A door slammed downstairs and I jolted awake, my first instincts to jump out of bed and check on Nathan. But as I threw back the covers, I noticed Jamison's muscled arm, slung over my abdomen, and the fact that I wasn't at home came rushing back. My eyes widened. Holy shit. I'd had a one-night stand.

The room was still that deep kind of black that let me know morning wasn't close yet, but streetlights let in some light, and my eyes adjusted quickly. I took in Jamison's bare skin and fought the urge to wake him and beg for round two. I was very aware of how naked we both still were, and round one had been amazing. A few awkward moments, but I hadn't had to fake that orgasm. I couldn't remember the last time Rick had bothered to make sure I enjoyed it as much as he did. And afterwards, Jamison hadn't just jumped up or made me feel like I should leave. He'd pulled me to him, resting my head on his bicep, and trailed his fingertips along my arm. And that was how I'd fallen asleep. Like a total one-night stand amateur. Which of course, is exactly what I was. Shit.

I lifted Jamison's outstretched arm and rolled away as slowly as humanly possible. My breath caught in my lungs, as I prayed he wouldn't wake up and make awkward small talk while I tried to find my underwear. I felt my cheeks burn at how horrifying that would be. How did people do this all the time?

Jamison stirred, and I froze as his arm snaked around my waist. "You don't have to go, you know." His lips pressed against my bare back in a move so tender my insides quivered.

I didn't know what to say. So I just went with the truth. "I didn't mean to fall asleep. I don't want this to be awkward."

"Then don't leave. 'Cos if I have to chase you out of here, begging for your phone number, *that* would be awkward. Especially because that was Mark coming in from work. He's seen me naked, but he doesn't particularly enjoy it."

I couldn't help but smile as I rolled over to face him.

"Come on, stay. It's three a.m. Where do you need to be at this time?"

I bit my lip. "You sure?"

He pulled me closer, so my ear rested on his chest. "Yeah. I am."

The next time I woke up, sunlight was streaming through the windows and I was completely alone in the bed. I rolled off the mattress and scooted around the floor looking for my clothes and underwear. I threw them on and stuck my head out into the hallway, checking left then right—coast clear. Barefoot, I padded downstairs, trying to make as little noise as possible. My high heels from last night still sat over by the front door, and for a second, I contemplated grabbing them and hightailing it out of there. But then I remembered the feel of Jamison's lips pressed to my shoulder, his chest against my back, skin touching skin. And I didn't want to leave without saying goodbye.

I poked my head around the corner of the empty living room, where a tiny dining room led to the equally small kitchen. My mouth dried at the sight of him sitting at the breakfast bar in only a pair of black fitted pants. His broad shoulders narrowed into a trim waist and he paused with a spoonful of cereal halfway to his lips. A slow smile spread across his face, lighting up his eyes.

"Hey! You're up," he slid off his stool and crossed the kitchen to pull the pantry door open. "Do you want some breakfast? We have Weet-bix? Or toast? There's probably bread in here somewhere."

He seemed genuinely pleased to see me. I tried not to read too much into that, though, pushing away the part of me that was thrilled with his reaction. He was a nice guy. Just because he was being nice to me this morning didn't mean he wanted anything more than what we'd had last night. It's not like I wanted anything more anyway. My life was too complicated right now to add anything more to it, even if his attention had come at exactly the right time.

Rick had kicked me when I was down, cheating with Bree, then marrying her so quickly after we'd divorced. I'd already picked myself up, but meeting Jamison last night had brushed off a little of the dirt that stubbornly clung to me.

I peered over at the bowl of half-eaten cereal he'd left on the bench. The milk was a chocolate swirl. "What are you having?"

He poked his head around the cupboard door. "Coco Pops. I know they're for kids, but I swear I eat like a grownup the rest of the day." A slight blush rose on his cheeks and he shrugged. "I like them."

He was adorable. And I was having trouble keeping my eyes off his abs. I internally high-fived myself for not leaving and missing out on the eye candy. I really had to go get Nathan, but he'd be fine with my mum until I got there. Nathan loved playing with the old Duplo blocks she'd kept from my childhood, and he'd be building castles while she fed him rubbish she would have never let me eat as a kid. Just a few more minutes to bask in my after-sex glow, then I'd go put on my mum face and pick him up.

I hooked one foot onto the footrest of the stool next to his and pushed myself up onto the seat. "You think I only buy Coco Pops for Nathan?" I raised an eyebrow and he grinned.

"Coco Pops it is then." He brought the box over to the bench and pulled a ceramic bowl and a spoon from the drawer beneath before pouring an unhealthy amount of the sugary goodness.

He slid back in the seat next to me, our arms brushing, as we ate in silence. From the corner of my eye, I saw him glance over at me a couple of times, and when I dared to do the same to him, our eyes met. Jamison smiled sheepishly, and a giggle escaped me. There was an awkwardness between us that hadn't been there last night, but it wasn't uncomfortable. It was actually kind of...sweet?

"I have to go to work, but I can drop you home on my way if you like?"

I found myself nodding, not wanting to leave him just yet. Memories of last night kept circling through my head on a never-ending loop—his jokes and laughing so hard my stomach hurt, the way he listened with his full attention to even the most mundane things I'd had to say. He'd rescued me from being the pathetic pushover who still showed up to her cheating husband's wedding. He'd turned a night I'd been dreading into a night I'd remember long after we said goodbye.

After he dumped his bowl in the kitchen sink, he pulled an ugly lavender shirt off the back of a dining room chair and pushed his arms through the holes, buttoning the shirt from the bottom up. I had to force myself not to voice my disappointment as his abs disappeared behind the buttons.

I shovelled the last few bites of cereal into my mouth, and when he'd finished tying his shoes, he held his hand out to me. "You ready?"

Nodding, I took his hand, unable to ignore the way my skin tingled as our fingers touched. I liked the way my hand felt in his. I liked the way my body tingled as he stood next to me. And I liked the memory of him touching me with care and longing all night. But I barely knew the man, beyond his name, and I knew I needed to stop romanticising everything. I was failing one-night stand 101 spectacularly.

He opened the car door for me and my insides went mushy. Again. Dammit. Did he always open doors for women? Was that part of who he was, or was he just on his best behaviour with me? In the confines of the car, his fresh, clean smell permeated the air, making me wish I'd asked if I could use his shower. My teeth felt furry and I probably reeked of smoke and alcohol and sex. Not a great combination.

It only took him a few minutes to drive to my place, his car pulling to a stop when I pointed out my two-storey modern brick house. The flowerbeds were all neatly tended, without a weed in sight, but my gaze narrowed in on a brown patch of grass near the letterbox. I made a mental note to make sure that spot got some extra water and maybe some fertilizer this week.

Jamison's forearm rested on the steering wheel, his other hand clutching the back of my seat as he gazed up at the brick monstrosity Rick and I had shared our entire married life. Rick had moved in with Bree when he'd left and hadn't fought me on it when I'd asked for it in the divorce. I planned to sell it and find something more "me"—something smaller and cosier. But Nathan had had enough upheaval in his life lately. A new house would have to wait until everything had settled down.

"So, thank you for last night." I unclicked my seatbelt, but my hand hovered over the door handle. "Not just the…uh, sex." Heat bloomed on my cheeks and I knew I was the one blushing now. "But for just hanging out and making the wedding bearable. Never in my wildest dreams did I think I would enjoy it. But I did."

Jamison's eyes raked over my face, but he didn't say anything, and I shifted in the silence. "Well, I guess I'll—"

"Go out with me, Elodie."

My stomach flipped, but I faltered in answering him. It was

one thing to spend the night with him, and for us to pretend this hadn't been a one-night stand as we'd sat eating breakfast together, but in the cold hard light of day, sitting outside the house I lived in with my child, I wasn't sure I should pretend any longer. Carrying this on any further would be such a bad idea. He was younger than me and unburdened by real-world problems. He still lived in the land of Uni assessments and a part-time job, while I felt years older than twenty-five and had a pile of baggage so high I could climb it like a ladder. I glanced up at the house again and tried to ignore the chant in my brain that screamed, "Say yes, you fool!"

"It's okay if you need to think about it." He pulled his phone out. "What if I just asked for your phone number instead?"

He looked so sweet and hopeful, and he'd been nothing but a gentleman from the minute we'd laid eyes on each other. He'd treated me with kindness and respect, and my hesitations were growing dimmer with every moment we sat here. With the memory of strong arms pulling me close in his bed, and whispered words of how sexy I was in the forefront of my mind, the last of my reserves crumbled. I nodded and held my hand out for his phone.

"I'd like that."

5

ELODIE

"S it down with those chips; you're dropping crumbs all through the house!" I yelled as Nathan tore past me in a blur of activity.

He stopped short and gave me one of his butter-wouldn't-melt grins. I frowned at him, but on the inside, I was smiling. "Go on, outside. And sit down before you choke." He scampered off, the screen door banging behind him, the excited barks of our dog Twister greeting him on the other side. I grabbed a Dust Buster and followed Nathan's crumb trail through the house.

I'd just turned the power off when the message tone on my phone beeped. I raced back to the kitchen and grabbed it off the bench.

Is it too early to ask you out again? Jamison

I sucked in a deep breath. It had been less than ten hours since he'd dropped me out the front of my house, and I'd spent nine hours and fifty-eight minutes of that time walking around smiling. *You're the sexiest woman I've ever had in my bed, Elodie,* played over and over in my head, and the memory of his lightly freckled skin against mine made me blush. The other two minutes had been spent cleaning up the chocolate milk Nathan had spilled all over me. But even spilled milk couldn't put a damper on my good mood.

I leaned on the kitchen bench and smiled at my phone. Why hadn't I just said yes to the date this morning? I'd wanted to. But Rick and I had only been separated a few months. I didn't need to be dating anyone new right now. I still had custody arrangements to finalise, and Nathan wasn't ready for me to have someone new in my life. I wasn't even sure if I was ready. Rick and I had been together for almost a decade. He might have cheated on me, but that didn't mean I was now completely devoid of all feelings for him. Real love didn't work like that. It wasn't just something you switched off one day. And I had loved Rick for a long time.

I really needed to just focus on Nathan, and myself. I cancelled out of the message, put my phone down, and pulled a packet of pasta out of the cupboard. Minced beef from the fridge, garlic, onions, tomatoes, stock, and spices appeared next, and I got busy making Nathan's favourite spaghetti bolognese for dinner. I had water bubbling in a saucepan and the tomato sauce simmering when my message tone sounded again. I pounced on it before the beeps had even finished, not even pretending to myself that I hadn't been hoping he'd message again.

How about now? J

A slow smile spread across my face. When was the last time a guy had flirted with me? I strained my brain to think of a single time and came up blank. Even when Rick and I had first gotten together, there had been practically no flirting. Rick had been a businessman, even as a teenager. He'd wanted me to go out with him, and I'd said yes. From then on, we'd just always been together. There had been no flirting. Not like I'd had with Jamison at the wedding last night. There'd been no cute text messages from Rick the day after we'd first slept together. Everything with him was planned out in advance, calculated. This thing with Jamison, if it really was even a *thing*, was completely different.

My phone buzzed in my hand and when I looked down he'd sent another message before I'd even closed out of the first one.

Tonight? Dinner?

I had Nathan and I'd already made dinner. I tried to ignore the sudden rush of disappointment as I typed back.

Sorry. Can't. I have Nathan and I've made spag bol.

I paused for a moment after I hit send, then quickly added. *Thank you for the invitation though.*

Oh well. That was that.

So why wasn't I putting the phone away?

I watched in some sort of stalker mode as the speech bubble appeared that signalled Jamison was writing a response. My breath caught in my chest and I blew it out in a long exhale. I couldn't deny I was dying to know what he would say. Guys like him—young, unattached, good-looking guys—didn't chase after women with kids and complicated relationships with their exes. But God, the low churning in my gut said I wanted his next message to be something more than *Okay, thanks anyway.* Was it too much to hope he'd chase me? Just a tiny bit?

I stared harder at the phone as the speech bubble disappeared, but no message arrived. Christ, had I insulted him by turning him down? That was the last thing I wanted. He'd been so kind to me.

Spag bol always tastes better the second night. Put it in the fridge and come out with me. Come on, Elodie. I'll beg if I have to.

Something that felt an awful lot like relief crashed over me. Why did I even care so much? *Because you really do want to go out with him, maybe?* A little voice in my head whispered. And the voice was right. I had every reason not to go out with him, but as soon as I'd said no, I'd wanted to take it back. The fact that I did have so many reasons not to get involved with him only made him all the more appealing.

I sighed. Then decided to be honest.

I really want to, but I have Nathan. Maybe next week after his dad is back from his honeymoon?

Jamison's reply came back almost instantly. *I don't want to wait that long to see you. Bring him with us?*

Oh. My. God. A heat began building low in my belly. He knew all the right things to say. Rick's lack of attention toward Nathan hadn't gone unnoticed by me. Or Nathan. So Jamison's opposing attitude was refreshing, if maybe a little premature. His kindness and consideration made me want to go more than ever. Only...I loved Nathan, but with heat washing over me from Jamison's words, Nathan was the last person I wanted to bring along on a date. I wanted to be me. Elodie. Not *just* Nathan's mum for a little bit longer.

Biting my lip, and feeling guilty, I rang my mum. She answered with her usual chirpy tone, and I pictured her settling into the wicker chair that she'd painted bright yellow, which sat by her phone cradle. She was one of the last people I knew to still have a landline, but she insisted she preferred it to the smartphone she carried grudgingly. She asked how Nathan was, and I answered before cutting to the chase.

"You know that guy I hung out with last night?"

"The cute one? I remember," Mum said with a laugh.

"He just asked me out."

"I'll be there to mind Nathan in fifteen minutes."

"Wait, what?"

"That's what you're ringing for, isn't it?"

"I feel really bad asking. You had him just last night—"

"And when was the last time you asked me to babysit before that? When was the last time you went out and enjoyed yourself?" Mum's tone shifted to one of frustration. "I can't even remember. Rick never bothered to take you anywhere, unless he needed to parade you around at one of his work functions."

My mouth dropped open. I knew Mum didn't particularly

like Rick, but I hadn't realised just how much until recently. The anger in her voice was evident.

"Plus, Nathan is my only grandbaby. I'm always happy to have him." A little of my guilt over leaving him for the second night in a row eased.

We hung up and I quickly typed a message back to Jamison.

No need, found a babysitter. What time are you picking me up?

YES! Be there in an hour.

6

JAMISON

*A*s Elodie and I approached the restaurant, I eyed the clear glass door, scanning it for a push or pull sign. I refused to be tripped up by something so simple on a first date. Grasping the handle, I pulled it toward me without incident and motioned for Elodie to go ahead. She smiled at me shyly as she passed, and I let my gaze roam over her back as she walked ahead to the hostess stand. The straps of the long dress she wore left her back exposed, the stretch of fair skin drawing my attention down her back to the soft swell of her ass. She looked just as good in clothes as she did out of them. I had to drag my attention away for fear I'd lean in to kiss and lick my way down her spine.

Instead I focused on the interior of the restaurant. It was fancier than most places I chose to eat, with white linen tablecloths and fresh flower centrepieces. I'd come here once before at Bree's request and had been surprised by how much I liked it. There were no burgers dripping with sauce and cheese fries, but their steak had more than made up for it. The food had been the only good thing about that night though. My memories turned sour as I remembered how we'd run into an old school friend of Bree's and spent a few minutes chatting with her. At the time, I'd thought everything was fine, but when we'd gotten out into the car, Bree had launched into attack mode, accusing me of flirting with the woman. That had been one of the first nights I'd realised how insecure and jealous she was.

"Table for two?" the hostess asked, jolting me out of my head.

I lifted my chin like they did in the movies, hoping it looked classy, and let my hand rest on the small of Elodie's back. My palm tingled as my skin came into contact with hers, and a slight shiver coursed through Elodie's frame.

"Are you cold?" The air-conditioning in the restaurant was pretty intense and I wished I'd brought a jacket I could drape around her.

She shook her head. "No, I'm fine." The thought that her shiver had been from my touch and not from the chilly air blasting around us gave me a burst of pleasure. If she was even half as affected by me as I was by her, we were off to a good start.

"Here you are. Your waiter will be right over," the hostess said with a smile after we followed her to a table. I pulled Elodie's chair out for her, and she slid into it, tucking her long skirt in around her.

"Thank you." She smoothed a white linen napkin over her lap and lifted her eyes to meet mine as I sat down across from her.

"Thank you for coming. I wasn't sure you would."

"I nearly didn't. But you were right when you said spaghetti is better the second night. It needs time for the flavours to really soak in. So it was either come out with you or starve."

I chuckled. "Can't have that."

"What would you have been doing if I'd stuck to my guns and eaten flavourless spaghetti tonight?"

I pondered her question for a moment. "Probably would have come here anyway. I started thinking about their steak at about ten this morning and haven't stopped thinking about it since."

A pink blush rose on Elodie's cheeks.

"What?"

"Nothing."

"No, tell me."

She studied her nails like they were suddenly the most interesting thing on the planet. "You spent all day thinking about food and I spent all day thinking about—"

The restaurant door opening again caught my eye, as a burst of noise from the street followed two new arrivals in. "Shit."

"What? Shit? I wasn't thinking about—" Confusion pulled her brows together.

I reached across the table and grabbed her hand as I slunk into my seat. "You will not believe who just walked in the door."

Elodie twisted in her seat, but I pulled her hand toward me and hissed. "Don't look!"

She sank into her seat an inch and leaned across the table, her expression as bewildered as if I'd just grown another head. "Are you going to tell me who it is we're hiding from?"

"Rick and Bree."

"What!" There was no stopping her spinning around to check out the couple speaking to the hostess. Her head flicked back to me, her eyes wide. "What are they doing here?! Rick told me he was on his honeymoon until next week! God, he is such a liar."

I shrugged. "Well unless they're honeymooning right here in Sydney..." I peeked over Elodie's shoulder and groaned.

"Busted. They've seen us."

Bree's eyes met mine and instantly narrowed into slits. I wanted to roll my eyes. I knew that look. I was in for it. I leaned in close to Elodie.

"Listen, I'm really sorry, but Bree is about to make a huge scene. Just ride the wave. She'll tire herself out quicker if we just agree with her." Elodie's eyes widened, her pretty mouth opening as if she wanted to say something. But Bree's high-pitched shriek broke glasses all over Australia, effectively silencing both Elodie and the entire restaurant.

"Jamison!" Bree stamped over, wearing fluro pink high heels

that had to be at least six inches tall, and judging from the look of pure, seething anger on her face, she was likely to pull one off and stab it through my eye. Rick trailed behind her, his eyes pinned on Elodie. Unease churned in my gut. Bree was all hot air and noise, but I didn't know this guy. And I didn't like the way Elodie shrank at my side. I forced a bright smile as Bree reached our table.

"Mr. and Mrs. Christoperson! How lovely to see you both. Is married life treating you well?" I knew I wasn't helping the situation by being a smart-ass but this was Bree through and through. Always finding a way to make every situation all about her.

"Don't give me that rubbish, you asshole. You ruined my wedding!"

I sobered up a bit, knowing antagonizing her further would only escalate the situation. And we probably did owe them an apology. "Look, Bree. I honestly am sorry. Elodie and I were just having a good time. We didn't mean to ruin anything."

"You didn't mean to ruin anything? Bullshit! You stole a microphone, sang some godawful karaoke, and made out with Rick's ex on a stage in front of three hundred people! Don't pretend you didn't know exactly what you were doing! You and this…" She trailed off as she looked over at Elodie, her venomous gaze sweeping over her from head to toe. Bree's lip curled and before I could move, she flung out one of her perfectly manicured hands and shoved Elodie hard in the shoulder. "This bitch!"

Elodie yelped as her chair rocked back, and I leapt up to put myself between the two women. Every eye in the room was on us, but I ignored them as I faced off with Bree. When I spoke, even I was surprised when my words came out as a low growl. "You don't touch her. Ever."

Bree laughed, the sound dark and cruel. "Or what?"

I glared down at her red face, recalling every jealous and destructive word she'd ever uttered when we'd been together. That night at the restaurant, when her jealousy had simmered its way to the surface, had only been the very beginning of our downhill slide. Maybe it was because there was never a true connection between us, and Bree knew it. Neither of us had ever said the L word, and her possessiveness and jealousy had only increased the longer we'd been together without either of us making a real commitment. She couldn't bear me speaking to other women, needing my complete and absolute attention and devotion at all times. I realised in that second that I'd inadvertently put Elodie in Bree's firing line, though I had a sneaking suspicion that, as Rick's ex, she'd been in it long before I'd come along. But I'd definitely made things worse. Bree might not have given a fuck about me anymore, but we'd stolen her thunder. And Bree wasn't one to just sit back and take that lightly. She'd bring heaven and earth down if she felt threatened. I couldn't let that happen.

She peered around me at Elodie even though her words were directed at me. "I've got her man. Her money. And it won't be long before that little boy is calling me Mummy." I heard Elodie gasp behind me.

"How do you like that, Princess?" Bree laughed nastily.

"Bree," Rick said weakly as he put his hand on her shoulder. She shrugged him off.

My blood boiled. "You're a piece of work, you know that? Go home."

Bree flicked her bottle-blond hair over her shoulder. "I couldn't stand to eat in the same restaurant as the two of you anyway." She turned on her heel and flounced toward the door. Rick's gaze lingered on Elodie for a long moment after Bree left, and I couldn't hold my tongue.

"Seriously, mate. That was fucked up. You have no problem with her speaking to the mother of your child like that?" I shook my head, unable to hide my disgust.

"Rick!" Bree screeched from the doorway, which seemed to startle Rick out of his thoughts and sent him chasing after her. I watched as they disappeared through the doors into the darkness of the night beyond, before I knelt down at Elodie's side.

"Shit, El. Are you okay?" I searched her face.

"I…I don't even know what just happened."

I grimaced as I took her hand.

"Nobody has ever shoved me like that before," she said slowly, rotating her shoulder. She looked up at me in confusion. "Did I deserve that? We did make a scene at their wedding."

I grasped the side of her face and waited until her gaze met mine. "You didn't deserve it. She's insane. We sang a bit of karaoke and we had a kiss. That's what people do at weddings."

Elodie shook her head and doubled over, leaning her elbows on her thighs. "What she said about Rick…and Nathan…" she clutched her stomach, and when she looked up at me, tears glistened in her eyes. "I have to leave my baby with that woman in a week's time."

My stomach rolled at the thought of any child being left in Bree's care. But I wasn't about to say that to Elodie. Instead I helped her to her feet. "She's too self-centred for kids. I doubt Nathan will even see her when he visits his dad. I promise, she only said that to hurt you."

We walked slowly to the front door, the eyes of the other people in the restaurant still boring holes in my back.

"Yeah, well, it worked."

ELODIE

I climbed gratefully into the passenger seat of Jamison's car and slammed the door. My heart still beat irregularly, but the interior of his car offered some sort of safety, at least from the stares and comments that had followed us out of the restaurant. Had that really just happened?

Regret swirled through me. I'd been angry at Rick for guilt-tripping me into going to the wedding. And Bree seemed to have some sort of lingering fascination with Jamison, even though I didn't feel it was reciprocated on his side. Jamison might have been right about us just doing what people did at weddings, but if I looked deep within me, hooking up with Jamison last night had at least partially been a fuck you to Rick and Bree.

Bree's words, *I've got her man. Her money. And it won't be long before that little boy is calling me Mummy* echoed through my head. I didn't give a shit about the money. I didn't make huge money at my job, but enough for Nathan and me to be comfortable. But she'd spoken about Rick like she owned him and that terrified me. He hadn't said a word. Would she be calling all the shots when it came to Nathan and Rick spending time together? And what about Rick and me? We had to have some sort of relationship in order to co-parent, but it didn't sound like Bree was planning to make that easy for me. If Rick allowed himself to be wrapped around her little finger, that was one thing. But Nathan...

Nathan had been my surprise baby. As had the extreme morning sickness I'd suffered when I was pregnant with him. For nine long months, I'd been in and out of the hospital, completely unable to work or study.

The hyperemesis gravidarum was why we'd never had any more kids.

Making that decision had been one of the hardest of my life, but I couldn't do another pregnancy like his. So I'd thrown myself into the role of wife and mother of a baby, then toddler, knowing I wouldn't get another chance. I wouldn't give him up to anyone without a fight.

Bile rose in my throat. I could only pray that Jamison's assessment of her threats had been accurate. I wanted Rick to have a relationship with his son, but God. Was she serious? Would she really try to take my son from me over one kiss with her ex?

Well, one kiss and some pretty decent sex. But she didn't know about that.

"Elodie?" I startled as Jamison's quiet voice brought me back to the present. "You're really quiet. Say something. Please."

"I just... How did you ever date her?" I leant my head back on the headrest and looked up at the ceiling of the car. God, I was tired. So, so tired.

"She isn't all bad."

I raised an eyebrow in his direction. "Could have fooled me."

He sighed and started up the car, manoeuvring it out of the car park and onto the road before he answered.

"I'd been ready to call it off after one particularly big argument, but then she'd told me about her sister."

I shifted on my seat so I could face him, headlights from other cars flashing by us as he drove. "She has a sister? I thought you said she didn't have any family?"

"No family that she speaks to. But she has got a sister. Story is that she ran off and married Bree's high-school sweetheart, so they don't speak."

"Wow. That's cold." Sympathy rolled through me, despite the way Bree had attacked me earlier and the way she'd run off with my husband. I couldn't help it. I didn't have any siblings, but I couldn't imagine not having any family. My mum had always been my rock, and I knew she'd be there, loving me, no matter what. How horrible it must feel to have no one watching your back.

"That was the only time she ever talked about her family. She'd been the ugly duckling as a kid, always lost in her sister's shadow. And then she'd thought the boyfriend was the real deal, but they'd run off together and left her with nothing. I felt bad for her."

"So, you stayed because you felt sorry for her?"

"No," he said quickly, surprising me with the depth of feeling behind the words. "I wouldn't just pity date someone. But I kind of understood her a little better after that, you know? She lost more than just her sister. She lost all of the self-confidence she'd managed to scrape up over the years. And she lost trust in men. Probably in women too, I guess. It'd be enough to make even the most confident person feel inferior."

He braked at a set of lights and reached out to take my hand. He squeezed it gently. "I thought there was a good person behind all her walls and self-destructive behaviour, and I wanted to find it. That's why I stayed."

Then he shrugged and gave me a wry grin. "But instead I'd found her in bed with Rick, and there was no coming back from that."

I laced our fingers together and when the light turned green, he drove with one hand instead of untangling himself. "I still don't get her fascination with you, though. She's moved on, married someone else, but she's still acting like a jealous girlfriend."

He chuckled. "It's not about me. It's you. You're the perfect wife and mother, El. She's trying to fill some pretty big shoes. She's young and insecure, and she hides it with aggression."

I gazed out the window at the dark night beyond without a single clue how to deal with that statement. I blew out a long breath. "I think I preferred when she was just the jealous ex." My brain hurt from trying to keep everything straight. I needed time to process everything. And sleep. Maybe everything would seem less dramatic in the morning. "Maybe we should just call it a night."

"You got it." Without hesitation, he flicked on a blinker and manoeuvred the car onto the main road that led to my house.

"But I'm hungry," I said, looking longingly at a KFC that flashed by all too quickly. It was late, and neither of us had eaten. I wanted to cry when I thought of the expensive steak that I could have been digesting right now if we hadn't had the unfortunate pleasure of running into our exes.

He chuckled. "Me too." There was silence between us for a moment before he said, "You know what? I can fix this."

Ten minutes later he pulled the car up in my driveway and turned off the ignition. We both got out and met in front of the car. Jamison handed me a brown paper bag that already had grease soaking the side. "It wasn't the fancy dinner I'd planned, but here. McDonald's chicken nuggets and chips aren't the worst alternative, right?"

I took them from him with a smile. "I told you in the drive-through, I love chicken nuggets. Sweet and sour sauce rules."

He screwed up his face. "Barbecue is better."

"We'll have to agree to disagree then." Silence fell over us and I looked down at my feet, not sure what to say. The date had been a disaster, and mummy guilt tugged at my heart. After Bree's horrible words, I needed to go see my little boy. But I didn't want to leave Jamison either. None of this had been his fault. He took my hand and led me to the front door. We stopped on the top step, and I squeezed his fingers. "I'd invite you in, but my mum is in there and she makes things awkward."

Jamison shook his head. "I wasn't going to ask. I just wanted to walk you to your door."

God, he was sweet. This wasn't how I wanted the date to end, but I knew it had to.

"Can I see you again? Try to make up for the disaster that was tonight? I promise to take you somewhere that none of my crazy exes will be."

Hope rose in my chest like fireworks. "I'd love that."

"Work is having a family fun day next weekend. Do you want to come? There'll be jumping castles and face painting and stuff?"

My heart thumped. "You want me to bring Nathan?"

He laced his fingers between mine and tugged me an inch closer. "Of course. They tend to frown on adults hogging the jumping castles." His grin faltered. "Unless you don't want me hanging out with him yet? I totally understand if—"

"No!" The words exploded from my lips before I could even think about them, but when I stopped to think about it, I found I didn't want to take them back. "I mean, no. I think it's really nice you want to bring him along. He loves that sort of thing."

Jamison's shoulders relaxed. "Good. I normally work at these functions, but Low, one of the guys on the bar staff, has had a lot of time off lately. I covered for him and he's still trying to make it up to me."

"So, I guess I'll see you next weekend then?" Disappointment flooded me when I realised it would be that long before we saw each other again.

Jamison frowned. "That's a really long time to wait to kiss you again."

"So kiss me now." The words sounded foreign on my lips, more bold and straightforward than I normally was, but I didn't want to wait a whole week to be in his arms again either.

He raised an eyebrow. "You do realise your mum is peeking out the window, right?"

I glanced over his shoulder just as one of the horizontal blinds fell back into place. I rolled my eyes and tilted my chin to look up at him. "I don't care if you don't."

He stepped closer, cupping my cheek with his hand and dipping his head so it hovered just above mine. "Cover your eyes, Barbara, you don't want to see this!" he called to my mother and dropped his lips to mine.

7

ELODIE

*L*ouise dropped a stack of contracts on my desk. The thunk as they filled my already full inbox tray wiped the smile right off my face. "Please tell me he doesn't want those finished today?"

Louise patted me on the shoulder. The pitying look that accompanied the gesture left no reason for her to verbally answer me. I sighed as I took out my elastic and ran my fingers through my hair, enjoying the brief feeling of freedom the simple task provided. Then I raked it back into a ponytail before I pulled the pile of papers closer. I hated when John, our CEO, dumped stuff on me last minute. But I never said no. If I worked hard, I might just be able to get through this lot without having to put in too much overtime.

The email alert on my computer pinged and a little flutter of excitement skittered through me. I hesitated for half a second, knowing I needed to tackle the mountain of work. But who was I kidding? I wouldn't be able to concentrate until I knew if that email was from Jamison.

I grabbed the mouse and clicked the alert. I wasn't supposed to take personal calls at work, so I'd given Jamison my email address earlier in the week. We'd sent a few quick emails to each other during our breaks, and even though they were completely tame—because who knew if the IT department were reading them as well—they always brightened my day. The idea of him thinking about me when we weren't together made my breath hitch. I couldn't wait to see him again on the weekend.

The screen switched to my inbox and my shoulders drooped. The email wasn't from Jamison. It was just an internal office memo from Louise, our office manager. I normally would have ignored it, with all the work I had piling up, but the subject line piqued my interest. *All Staff Formal Charity Dinner.* I skimmed the email. John had lost his wife to brain cancer a few months earlier and it seemed the company wanted to do something in a show of support. I nodded to myself, as I jotted the details down in my planner, and smiled when I noticed it was being held in the function room at Jamison's work. John's wife had been a lovely woman, and I'd heard she'd been very sick in the end. I wanted to do my part and show my support. He may have loved to dump work on me late in the day, but he'd always been a kind and fair employer, and nobody deserved to lose a loved one to such a cruel disease.

I picked up my bag to put my planner away only to find my bag vibrating. I fumbled through it until I found my phone, flashing with an incoming call. It diverted to voicemail before I could grab it, and that's when I noticed I had five missed calls, all of them from Nathan's school.

The next few minutes were a whirlwind of shoving papers into my bag, calling apologies to my co-workers, and waiting for an impossibly slow lift, all with my heart in my mouth. Because something had to be wrong. Nathan's school didn't call for no reason. He was either sick or injured, and since he'd been completely healthy when I'd dropped him off this morning, I'd immediately begun picturing broken bones and cuts that needed stitches.

The receptionist finally picked up my call as the lift arrived with its artificial binging noise.

"Ms. Chalmers? Nathan is just fine."

A breath of relief whooshed out of me and I leant heavily on the wall of elevator. Thank God he wasn't hurt. Then why the five— "It was Principal Deans that called you. Are you able to come in for a meeting this afternoon? It's quite urgent. We'd like Mr. Christoperson to come in as well."

The lurch in my stomach didn't have anything to do with the elevator rapidly dropping floors. "Yes, of course. I'm on my way. Don't call my ex-husband though. He's on his honeymoon."

"As you wish. Just come to reception when you get here."

I nodded, even though there was no one in the elevator to see it, thanked her, and ended the call.

Forty minutes later, I pulled up outside of the pale brick buildings that made up Nathan's school. The gardens were neatly tended, and the school fields were thick with lush-looking grass. It had an air of class about it, which was exactly why Rick had been adamant that we enrol Nathan there. I'd agreed, impressed by the school's academic results. But I didn't much care for the fancy uniforms or the school fees that cost us a few thousand dollars each year. Gossip ran rife in the parent cliques, which I knew would eventually filter down to the kids. And I'd heard more than one whisper about Rick and me over the past few months. I felt out of place there, now that I wasn't part of a perfect little nuclear family. More than once, I'd thought about switching him to the local public school, which also had a fantastic reputation. Public schooling hadn't hurt either Rick or myself. But I knew Rick liked the prestige, and Nathan had made friends. Now wasn't the time to rock the boat with Rick, and I just wanted Nathan to be happy and settled. I hurried into the front office, my low heels clicking on the polished cement floors.

The aboriginal woman on the other side of the door looked

up and greeted me with a smile as I approached. "Ms. Chalmers? Mrs. Deans is waiting for you. Go right on through."

I swallowed hard and pulled my shoulders back, straightening my posture. Why did I suddenly feel like I was the one that was in trouble?

I knocked on the door marked with the principal's name and waited for her to call me in. The door swung open and the tall woman on the other side offered me her hand to shake. I took it, forcing a smile across my face so she wouldn't notice how nervous I was. At twenty-five years old, this was the first time I'd ever been summoned to a principal's office. Maybe Nathan was getting some sort of award? Something deep inside me told me that was somehow unlikely.

"Reception told me Mr. Christoperson couldn't come. That's a shame, because this is something I wished to discuss with the both of you. But it's urgent, so I don't think waiting for him to return is advisable."

I shook my head. "It's fine. The two of us are divorced, but we're on...good terms." Good enough terms anyway. "I'll fill him in on whatever the problem is."

She nodded curtly, as we both took seats. She jotted something down in a file, and I had to force myself not to peer over the desk to see what she'd written. I crossed my legs and waited for her to begin.

"Nathan was in a fight on the playground today."

"What?!" My stomach rolled. "The receptionist said he was fine. Where is he? Is he hurt?"

The woman shook her head. "No, he's fine. He's in class. The thing is, he's the one that instigated the fight. He attacked another little boy."

"I'm sorry. Excuse me?" I shook my head slowly, trying to make sense of her words. "He attacked someone? Are you sure? He's not an aggressive kid. He's never hurt anyone before." My chest tightened. "Who was the other child? Are they okay?"

Nathan wasn't perfect. I knew that, but he was a damn good kid. He was polite and caring and the school had regularly given him awards for outstanding behaviour. The words rolling out of the principal's mouth didn't compute with the little boy that had wrapped his skinny arms around my neck a few hours earlier and told me I was the most beautiful mum he'd ever had.

"We can't discuss the other child with you unfortunately, but medical care was required. So we're taking the matter very seriously."

"Oh my God." I scrubbed my hands over my face, wishing the ground would swallow me up. "Are you expelling him?"

I barely dared to look at the principal, but when I did, she was shaking her head.

"No, we aren't. Nathan was one of our best students last year, and his teacher has expressed her shock over the events that took place today. But she did also say that he's been quiet in class recently, and not participating in games or activities at lunchtime either. After his outburst today, we're concerned. Have you noticed any of this sort of behaviour at home? Have there been any big changes in his life lately?"

I shook my head slowly. "His father and I divorced, and Rick remarried recently. So, there's been some disruption to his regular routine, I suppose. He seemed okay with it all, though..." The principal folded her hands before launching into a speech about how divorce and family dynamics can adversely affect a child's learning. My head bobbed up and down, agreeing with her, but my brain checked out.

Nathan had barely seen Rick since he'd left. Bree and Rick had picked him up a handful of times to take him out for the day, but we hadn't sorted out a proper custody arrangement yet. He'd been so busy with Bree and the wedding that I hadn't pushed him to see Nathan, preferring not to speak to Rick if I didn't have to. I'd been content to keep Nathan all to myself.

I hadn't made an effort either, and the only person that hurt was Nathan. And now, after the scene at dinner, who even knew where things stood between Rick and me. Bree's hateful words replayed in my head. *I've got her man. Her money. And it won't be long before that little boy is calling me Mummy.* This whole situation had gotten out of control.

When Rick had left I'd sworn to myself I wouldn't let it affect Nathan. I'd sworn to maintain a friendship with him, despite the way he'd hurt me, and that together we'd always put Nathan first. Did he sense the way I resented his father and his actions? I thought I'd hidden that from him, but maybe I wasn't doing a good enough job. I knew he missed his dad. But I'd thought it wasn't much different from the times Rick had missed dinners or his soccer games. A band tightened around my chest, making it difficult to breathe.

The principal folded her hands on her desk and nodded. "When I questioned Nathan about the incident he said he threw the chair because the other child said he didn't have a dad."

I felt the blood drain from my face. "He threw a chair? Oh my God." Tears pricked at the back of my eyes. "I'm so incredibly sorry. I'll... I'll sort this out. It won't happen again." I just wanted to get out of there so I could let the tears spill over. The guilt swirling through me morphed into a chant that clouded out all other thought. This was all my fault. Mine and Rick's. Nathan was six years old. His behaviour was a direct product of the decisions Rick and I made for him. And we'd both been thinking more about our love lives than what was going on with our son. We'd really dropped the ball.

8

JAMISON

*D*irt gathered in a neat little pile as I pushed the broom halfheartedly across the tiled floor of the bar. End-of-shift cleaning sucked. And Low was making it worse by being annoying. I less than subtly nudged at his feet, which were firmly planted in my way, as he stood making out with his girlfriend, Reese. Her long dark hair fell down her back as he pulled her tight against his chest and melded his mouth to hers. I rolled my eyes. Apparently they couldn't keep their hands off each other long enough to make it through end-of-shift cleaning.

As much as I loved them both—Low was my best friend and Reese and I were tight too, in a brother/sister kind of way—their constant PDA was enough to roll even the strongest of stomachs. And right now, they were holding me up. I just wanted to get home so I could call Elodie.

"Sorry, Jam," Reese said, kissing me quickly on the cheek before stepping aside. "We'll stop. I swear."

I instantly felt bad. I didn't begrudge them their happiness. But being around it every day did reinforce that I wanted a little of it for myself. After the rubbish with Bree, and with my graduation and my real life looming, I was ready for something different. Something real. Something meaningful. Maybe Elodie wasn't the person I'd find that with—it was too early to tell—but I wanted the chance to find out. She was beautiful and sweet and kind. The complete opposite of the women I normally dated. And I liked it. She was a glimmer of reality in the ocean of fake.

"No, it's okay. I'm in a mood. If Elodie were here, I'd be happy to stand here and make out with her instead of cleaning as well."

Reese leant a hip back on the bar, tucking her fingertips into her pockets as she regarded me. "You really like her, huh?"

I tapped the broom on the floor as an excuse to look at the floor and avoid making eye contact with her. I knew I was probably blushing. "She's different."

I glanced over at her just in time to see Reese give Low a look I couldn't identify. But the two of them smiled as if they held all the secrets of the world. They'd gone through so much to be together, and despite their rocky start, were now more in sync than some couples who'd been together for years. I'd never had that sort of all-consuming connection, and even from the outside looking in, I could tell how special it was.

Elodie and I had been emailing all week, but she hadn't answered the email I'd sent earlier in the day. I'd spent all afternoon thinking about it, wondering if I should email again, or maybe send a text message. It'd already been a few days since I'd seen her, and I just wasn't good at playing it cool when I wanted something. And whatever this was between Elodie and me, it was something. Part of me hoped it might even be something like what Reese and Low had found. Bree and I had never really committed to each other, even after six months of dating. But here I was, less than two weeks after meeting Elodie, wondering if this was more than just a fling. I decided to call her after work.

I waited until eight, so she'd have time to put Nathan to bed, before I flopped on my lounge and scrolled through my phone to her name.

"Hey," she said softly after the third ring.

"Hi," I said tentatively. She didn't sound happy. "Is this a bad time?"

"No, no. I just had a rough day."

"Want to talk about it?" It was a throwaway line I'd used on people before, even when I'd had no interest in what they'd been doing. But with her, I found myself honestly wanting to know exactly what had her so down. I wanted to know everything about her. I wanted to know what made her happy and what made her sad. I wanted to know what made her answer the phone sounding as if the weight of the world was on her shoulders.

"Nathan threw a chair at someone today."

"What?!" I choked out. That had been the last thing I'd expected her to say. The kid was tiny! How could he even pick a chair up?

"That was my reaction too. I think he's acting out because of the divorce."

I picked at a thread on a cushion while I pondered that. "Lots of people get divorced, though. You can't just blame yourself."

There was a muffled sound before she replied. "Maybe not *just* me."

I frowned, but I didn't know what to say to make this better for her. I had no experience with kids or parenting or parenting with an ex. I was wholly unqualified to be a participant in this conversation, even though I desperately wanted to ease some of the sadness in her voice.

"What did Rick say?"

She snorted. "I assume he's overseas somewhere. I sent him a text message telling him what happened, but he didn't write back. He probably has no phone reception."

"That sucks. Sorry you had such a shitty day, El. I wish I could make it better for you."

"You did." She paused, before adding in a small voice, "Just hearing your voice makes me feel better."

Relief inflated my lungs. I loved hearing those words on her lips. I toyed with the idea of offering to come over there and make her feel better in a whole different sort of way. But she sounded tired and I didn't want to intrude. So instead, I settled for the reason I'd called. "Are we still on for the fun fair on the weekend?"

There was a long silence before she responded. "I probably shouldn't take him. His behaviour today doesn't exactly warrant a treat."

Shit! This wasn't going the way I wanted it to.

"But...? Please tell me there's a 'but' coming. I really want to see you." I couldn't help the hopeful tone my voice took on, though I desperately wanted to sound cool and calm. I'd been counting down the minutes until I got to see her. If she cancelled now, who knew how long it would be before I'd get to see her again. Even an extra five minutes was too long when we'd already been apart all week.

She chuckled into the mouthpiece. "But I did already take away his iPad and he's going to sit on the sidelines and cheer for his soccer team for the next two weeks instead of playing. So maybe that's enough." She sounded more like she was trying to convince herself than explain things to me. "He's been counting down the days to the fair; he'd be devastated to miss it. And I'd rather focus on positive reinforcement than negative."

A grin lifted my frown. "That sounds reasonable. He's just a kid. I doubt it was a thought-out, premeditated attack."

"Let's hope so. I'll see you Saturday."

I fist pumped the air so viciously I was surprised I didn't pull a shoulder muscle. I was also thankful she couldn't see me. Because there was nothing cool or calm about how excited I was to spend more time with her.

ELODIE

There wasn't a cloud in the sky when I cracked open my bedroom blinds on Saturday morning. A little part of me had been hoping it would rain and the fun fair would be cancelled. It would have been the only thing to save me from the tormented tug of war that had been tearing me apart since Nathan's school dilemma.

I wanted to see Jamison. Every sweet word he'd ever said to me made my heart sing as loudly as a choir. The way I felt when he touched me or kissed me made every nerve ending buzz. But I'd lain awake thinking for the majority of the past two nights, guilt and confusion grating at my happiness. I'd thought things through for hours, and still didn't have any concrete answers. On one hand, I had this super sweet, super hot guy I was really into. A guy who elicited feelings in me I hadn't felt for years. While on the other hand, I had my son, my ex, and the disaster that was Bree. Carrying on things with Jamison wouldn't help the situation there. Nathan was struggling and my deteriorating relationship with his father would only make that worse. I should have cancelled the date, but I'd selfishly convinced myself that Nathan had been looking forward to it. But I knew it was me that had been looking forward to it the most. Maybe if we just took things super slow, and everyone had time to adjust...

In an effort to look nice at the fun fair, but still remain practical, I'd decided on a singlet top and a long multi-coloured skirt, and matched it with flat, comfortable sandals. It was summery and pretty, and I'd been pleased with my reflection in the mirror this morning. All had been fine as Nathan and I made our way through the racecourse turnstiles and out onto the track where all the action was. But we'd been taking in the carnival atmosphere when he'd gone shy, grabbed hold of my skirt, and spun it around himself. He'd effectively become cocooned in the fabric. Of course, Jamison chose that moment to appear through the crowd. I desperately grabbed at the loose elastic waistband to keep Nathan from pulling it straight off my hips. The several hundred people milling around the tracks didn't need to see my underwear.

Jamison stopped in front of me and glanced down at the Nathan-shaped lump in my skirt. My heart skipped a beat at the sight of him.

"Hi." I waved, relieved but also a tiny bit disappointed when he didn't try to kiss me. I rubbed Nathan's head through his makeshift hiding spot. "Nate, do you want to come say hi to my friend Jamison? You met him at the wedding. He's very nice."

Nathan shook his head against my legs and I shrugged at Jamison. "He's a bit overwhelmed."

Jamison crouched down and spoke to my skirt lump. "It's okay, mate. I don't like talking to strangers either. But is it alright with you if I talk to your mum and show her around?"

A man wearing a Lavender Fields uniform approached us and clapped Jamison on the shoulder, but Jamison didn't move from his crouched position. "There's lots of fun stuff to do here today, like jumping castles and swinging chairs and water fights…"

Nathan didn't respond, only wrapped himself tighter in the material.

"Or he could come see the foals," the other man said.

Jamison glanced up at him and raised an eyebrow. "Yeah?"

He straightened his long body into a standing position again and reached for my hand. I let him link his fingers through mine, trying to ignore the pleasant warmth that cascaded from his palm to mine. "Elodie, this is Low. Low, Elodie," he said, motioning between us. Low offered me his hand and I shook it with a smile.

"Nice to meet you, Elodie. Jamison hasn't shut up about you all week."

Jamison shot Low a look, making him chuckle, before he knelt back down. "Hey, Nathan? Do you like horses? Low has a really cute one out the back I want to show you."

Nathan poked his head around my legs. "Is it a boy horse? I only like the boy ones."

Jamison nodded. "Just so happens it is. What's your favourite colour?"

Nathan took a tiny step to the side. "Blue."

Jamison scratched his chin. "Damn. Well, the foal isn't blue, but he is a really cool colour. He's all black."

"I like black too."

"Yeah? Me too. Bet you can't guess his name?"

Nathan put his little hands on his hips in defiance and I choked back a laugh. "Bet I can!"

I gave Jamison a subtle thumbs up. He winked and held out a hand to Nathan. "Well, come on then. I'll show you where he is. I'll bet you a dagwood dog you can't guess his name before we get there." My mouth watered at the thought of the deep-fried carnival food. I'd been too conflicted to eat breakfast that morning and my stomach was rumbling. Nathan looked up at me for permission and I nodded. His little fingers wrapped around Jamison's hand and the two of them walked with Low through the crowd, Nathan throwing out name suggestions in rapid fire.

I lagged behind. Warmth threatened to flood my heart as I watched Jamison win my child over, step by step. Shit. I needed to pull the reins in on this before I got fully swept away.

"Bob? Scratch? Thunder?" Nathan's curious guesses washed back to me on the summer breeze, along with the smells of deep-fried carnival food.

Jamison shook his head. "Nope, but Thunder was kind of in the right direction."

"Lightning? Storm?"

"Nope."

"Give me a hint?" Nathan wheedled.

"Well, you're kind of right, going down the nature path. But he's black, so…"

I bent down and whispered in Nathan's ear. He frowned at me. "Onyx? What's that?"

Jamison chuckled. "Don't listen to your mum. She's wrong!"

Now it was my turn to frown as Low walked a few paces away and scanned a security card that popped open a gate. I pondered Jamison's clues as we followed Low through, and he closed it firmly behind us. I whispered in Nathan's ear again.

"Midnight!" he yelled.

Jamison stopped short. "Seriously? Now I owe you a dagwood dog."

"Yes!" Nathan cheered. "Told you I could guess it!"

I chuckled and ruffled his hair, pleased that he'd come out of his shell. It only worsened my confusion about Jamison and me though. If he'd hated Jamison, it would have been easier to slow this down or even end it. The fact they were getting along made me want more days like today. Trips to the beach and board game nights and camping trips. Just the three of us. It would be all too easy to jump into this thing head first, without thinking through the consequences. And if we carried on, the way we had been, there would be consequences.

Beyond the racecourse gates were acres of training and holding paddocks, along with multiple large buildings. Low pointed to the largest of them. "That's the main stables over there. All the out of town horses stay there when there's big races on, but it's pretty empty right now. Things get a bit quiet in the summer, after the rush of the Spring Racing Carnival."

"Wow. This place is amazing," I breathed, allowing myself a minute to let my guard down and just appreciate my surroundings. I'd never seen anything like Lavender Fields. It was an oasis in the middle of an otherwise suburban city area.

"I've got to go check in with the stable hands, but you guys go on ahead. I'll catch up with you later on."

Jamison slapped his hand against Low's, and Nathan and I both waved.

Jamison led us to a paddock fence and hoisted Nathan up to the middle rail so he could see over the top. He pointed to a shiny black foal that was busy galloping across the paddock with his gangly, still uncoordinated legs. "That's Midnight."

One of the little horse's ears twitched, and he suddenly dropped to the ground and rolled in the dirt.

Nathan's little kid giggles were infectious. "He's so cute! Can I ride him?"

"Not yet, he's not strong enough to carry a big guy like you. Maybe when he's as big as that horse over there. That's his mum. And see that bigger one at the back? She's his big sister." Jamison pointed out each horse as he spoke.

"How do you know all this? I thought you worked in the bar?" I asked Jamison curiously.

"I do, but these ones belong to Low and Low's grandparents. I went with him yesterday to pick them up from their property and bring them here for the day. They wanted to have some young ones out for the kids to look at when they do stable tours as part of the afternoon events."

"Ah."

Nathan climbed down off the fence and picked up a short stick. He crouched in the dirt and wrote his name in crooked letters.

"Want to go do the jumping castles and get that dagwood dog now?" Jamison asked him.

Nathan nodded enthusiastically and grabbed Jamison's hand again. But when we got to the jumping castles, Nathan went shy. "There's lots of big kids on there..." Disappointment filled his voice.

"So?" Jamison asked.

"He's worried they'll jump on him," I filled in.

Jamison frowned. "Come on then, I'll jump with you. I'm twice as big as those kids."

Nathan beamed up at him. "Yeah! You are really big!"

I raised an eyebrow in Jamison's direction. "I thought you said the jumping castles weren't for adults?"

He put on an over-the-top sleazy voice and said, "It's all about who you know, baby."

I rolled my eyes as he toed off his shoes and slung a shrieking Nathan over his shoulder. Nathan's giggles filled the air as Jamison jogged across the small stretch of grass to the inflatables. My heart felt as if it was being cracked wide open. Was he really this into kids, or was this just a way of impressing me? Either way, it was working. I tried hard not to think about what an amazing dad he'd be, but it was a losing battle. He was a natural.

"Well, that's adorable."

I jumped at the voice so close to me, and the dark-haired woman next to me did the same thing.

"Oh, sorry." She put her hand on my arm. "I didn't mean to sneak up on you. I'm Reese; I'm Low's girlfriend. And I work with Jamison at the bar. You're Elodie, right?"

I nodded. I guess Low hadn't been joking when he said Jamison had spoken about me during the week.

"I've only got a minute left of my break, but I saw you guys over here and I had to come introduce myself." She nodded in Jamison's direction. "I've never seen him around kids. I didn't realise he was so good with them." Jamison lifted Nathan onto the castle, then with a wave at the attendant, took a running leap onto the castle himself, bouncing high enough to hit his head on the roof, which made Nathan double over with fresh rounds of laughter.

"He's been great today. Amazing, really. I think Nathan likes him a lot." I didn't voice my conflicted feelings over that.

Reese's wide smile lit her eyes. She was pretty. She and Low would be a stunning couple, side by side. "They look like they're having a ball."

I smiled as Nathan followed Jamison around the jumping

castle like a lost puppy, his floppy blond hair falling in his eye with every jump.

Reese glanced over at me. "What about you? Are you enjoying getting to know him?"

I startled, which made Reese laugh. "Sorry, that was forward, wasn't it? He's my friend, and I know he likes you."

The question had taken me by surprise, but I shook my head. Reese exuded warmth and kindness. Her blunt question had obviously come from a good place. "It's okay. I like him too," I said cautiously. That was the truth. Dammit. Why did this all have to be so complicated?

"It's good to see him have some fun. He's spent all his time working lately. Low and I both had a lot of stuff going on, and Jamison really picked up our slack."

"Everything okay now?" I asked cautiously.

She nodded, her long, brown hair bouncing in her ponytail. "It's great." She looked at her watch. "Crap, I have to go, my break is over. Can you tell Jam I said hi?"

She waved as she walked away toward the main building. "Oh hey, Elodie?" she called, turning back. "Let's double date some-time, okay? Dinner and a club, maybe? I'll organise something with Jamison."

I smiled, not sure how to answer. Reese couldn't have been that much younger than I was, but she had a carefree vibe about her I knew I lacked. I wasn't just free to do whatever I wanted, whenever I wanted. I had a son and responsibilities, and those things were important to me. I didn't resent them at all, but they did mean I wasn't free to just do whatever I wanted. My whole life revolved around doing the right thing for Nathan. Going out for a night of partying wasn't just a simple thing. It required planning and babysitters and most likely staying sober because who could deal with a six-year-old with a hangover. The best thing for me wasn't necessarily the best thing for him. I'd accepted that the minute I'd first held him in my arms. Reese and

Low seemed lovely, but I wasn't sure I'd fit in with Jamison's crowd. I wanted to, but I felt years older than them all. Reese seemed to take it as a given though and disappeared into the crowd.

I turned back to the jumping castle, just as Nathan and Jamison climbed off and ran back to plop down on the grass at my feet. "Hi, Mum!" They both picked up their shoes and tugged them on. Nathan's cheeks were red, and he was puffing, but his eyes gleamed.

"Hey, buddy. How was that?"

"Awesome! Jamison is teaching me how to do front flips!"

I squinted at Jamison. "Is he now?"

Jamison grinned and brushed his lips against my cheek, his slight stubble rasping across my skin. It was the most simple and innocent of touches, and yet time seemed to stand still when he was close to me. His cologne mixed with his natural man scent drifted around me, and I fought the urge to turn into him and kiss him the way I really wanted to. "He twisted my arm. And I was watching him the whole time. Swear."

"Mmmmm hmmm." As he slung his arm around my shoulder, his fingers brushing the bare skin of my arm, I felt the last of my reserves crumble. I gave into the temptation to just be in the moment. We'd need to talk about this later, talk about slowing this way down. But for now, I let happiness settle over me, even if it was probably temporary.

"Dagwood dog time, Nathan?"

"Yeah!"

I snaked my arm around Jamison's middle and turned my face up to him. With a quick glance to make sure Nathan wasn't paying attention, he dropped a kiss to my lips. This was turning out to be a much more successful date than the last one we'd been on.

9

JAMISON

*N*athan jumped on the lounge, the springs creaking beneath his little feet every time he hit the cushion. "Look, Jamison!" He raised his hands and I caught him mid jump, setting him down on the ground.

"Hey mate, I know you're super good at those front flips, but I think Mum might get angry if you're doing them on the lounge. Don't you think?"

He tucked his blond hair behind his ear and stuck his bottom lip out. "Yeah, I guess so."

"Right answer," Elodie said as she came back into the room. I cringed and mouthed the word *sorry* whilst giving her my best puppy dog eyes. She shook her head, her hair swishing around her face. "Nate, it's time for bed. Say good night to Jamison, please."

"Good night, Jamison. Thanks for teaching me front flips!"

I ruffled his hair as he ran by me to his mum's outstretched hand. "Good night, mate. Next time we'll work on backflips."

Nathan cheered and Elodie shot me an exasperated look.

Oops.

I straightened all the cushions on the lounge, because I knew it would bother Elodie to see them all over the place in her otherwise perfectly spotless living room. I flicked the TV onto a tennis match, but nervous energy made me too jumpy to just sit on the lounge and watch it. So, instead, I paced around the living room as I waited for Elodie to put Nathan to bed. Every photo frame on every wall held photos of Nathan at various ages, and his artwork was displayed proudly on wall clips. I bypassed the family photos that included Rick.

Even after spending all day with Nathan and Elodie, I hadn't had enough. Playing with Nathan had been a ton of fun, but he'd been the centre of my attention. Just being in Elodie's presence hadn't quenched the thirst that had developed over the world's longest week. Emailing wasn't enough, and being with her today, but not really being allowed to touch her or talk to her about anything other than which ride to go on next, had been a sweet agony. It had only drawn out the pull I'd felt, and I couldn't wait to get her alone.

From the bedroom Elodie's voice rose up, sweet and calm, as she sang Nathan a lullaby. Her voice was beautiful, easy, and flowing, and I closed my eyes for a moment just to listen. She was a good mum. I'd never dated anyone with kids before, but I had three nieces and a nephew. I liked kids. I certainly didn't want any of my own right now, not when I was so close to finishing Uni and actually being able to start a real career, but I had no problem with other people's.

Elodie didn't need to tell me the two of them were a package deal. I knew it from the first moment I'd seen them sitting together at the wedding. The way she smiled at him when he wasn't looking. The gentle way she touched him. I instinctively knew she'd do anything for that little boy. He was always going to be her number one priority and that was how it should be. I didn't need kids of my own to understand that.

But I hoped she had room in her life for something more.

Elodie padded back into the living room on bare feet and leant on the doorway. A small smile played over her lips and her hair was mussed up on one side from where she'd lain with Nathan. "Who's playing?"

She still wore the long skirt she'd had on at the racecourse, but she'd hiked it up to mid-thigh and tied it in a knot on one side, so she wouldn't trip on the hem without sandals on. My eyes travelled up the length of her leg, over the flare of her hip, to the narrowing of her waist. "I don't know."

Elodie laughed. "You've been out here watching it for fifteen minutes and you don't know who's playing?"

I shrugged. "I think I forgot my own name when you walked out here looking like that." She bit her lip, something I was coming to recognise she did when I said something she liked. "Is Nathan asleep?"

She nodded.

"Then why the hell are you all the way over there?"

She crossed the space, until she stood in front of me, then pushed me gently, urging me backwards until my calves hit the lounge. I sat, the lounge creaking as it accepted my weight, and Elodie's hair fell around her face in a waterfall as she stood over me. My heart hammered in my chest at the look of lust and need that swirled in her expression. I knew it was probably mirrored in my own.

My fingers found and travelled up the smooth length of leg she had on display, stopping just under the knot she'd tied. I gave it an experimental tug, watching as the waistband slid down her hip an inch, exposing a sliver of skin between her skirt and top. I leant forward and brushed my lips over the space. Her body swayed before she lowered herself to kneel in the space between my legs. Heat flashed in her eyes as they met mine. I lifted one hand and slid it along the side of her face, so my fingertips curled into her hair. My other hand found her hip, my thumb brushing over the sliver of skin my lips had kissed just moments earlier. I don't know if I leant in, or if she was the one to narrow the gap between us, but our lips hovered inches away.

"Thank you for today," she whispered.

"You're welcome." My eyes dipped to her mouth. Soft and pink. She'd worn lipstick earlier in the day, but it had long worn off. Her tongue darted out to run over her lips and I fought back a groan.

"There's something really sexy about a man that likes kids, you know?"

I chuckled. "No, not really. But if you're calling me sexy, I'll take it."

"You're sexy, Jamison."

"Yeah?"

"Mmmhmm." She swept her lips over mine, and my grip tightened on her hip. "Really damn sexy."

Her lips returned, her tongue immediately seeking to deepen the kiss. I couldn't hold back the groan I'd been supressing as her tongue found mine. My fingers tightened in her hair as I slid forward on the lounge and pulled her close to me. Her lips were demanding, controlling the pace and intensity of the kiss and I followed her lead. Her hands palmed my thighs, inching higher up my legs, my cock thickening with every centimetre her fingers covered. She pulled back, giving me a little smile before she looked down and flicked open the fly of my shorts.

"Stand up," she whispered. I obeyed, my shorts falling down my legs without the support of the button and fly. My cock strained behind my boxer briefs, begging to be set free. Her gaze lingered on my dick, and my heartbeat picked up. My stomach rolled in anticipation.

Elodie's fingers trailed along the waistband of my briefs, before she slid them down, just low enough to free my cock. It sprung out, thick and hard, and her gaze lifted to mine as her pink tongue shot out and circled the head. *Shiiiit.*

I was almost as surprised as she was when I put a hand on her cheek and stopped her from lowering her mouth over me.

"Wait, El. Nathan…"

She shook her head. "Once he's asleep, he's out cold. We won't hear from him until morning."

I relaxed a little, though the thought of his little blond head poking around the corner as his mother bobbed over my dick was horrifying. Elodie's hot mouth closed over me, heat spreading through me like wildfire. Her hand wrapped around the base, following her mouth as she slid over me, her tongue stroking the sensitive underside. My hand fisted in her hair, but I wasn't controlling her. This was her show. Her tongue swirled around me again and pleasure rolled through me, but…

Fuck.

I couldn't stop thinking about Nathan just down the hallway. It was making me paranoid and distracting me from the warmth of her mouth. Which is exactly what I really wanted to be focusing on.

"El, stop."

Her head lifted, her eyes slightly unfocussed. "What's wrong? You don't like it?" Her eyebrows drew together, and embarrassment flickered in her eyes. The alpha male in me loved that she wanted to please me. That was hot.

"Fuck, no. I love it. I just don't want to do this here. Nathan…"

Her sigh stirred a loose hair at the side of her face. "I understand." She sat back on her heels and pushed to her feet. As she moved away, I saw the disappointment in her eyes.

Yanking up my shorts, I chased after her and spun her around, her body crashing against mine.

"I didn't mean we should stop altogether, El. Where's your bedroom?"

The edges of her mouth turned up. "Down the hall. Next to Nathan's room."

"Fuck!" My cock throbbed at how close she was.

Mischief glinted in her eyes. "The bathroom is at the back of the house, though. And it has a lock..."

Fuck. Yes.

With my head rushing, I followed her down the hall, tiptoeing when she looked back at me and placed a finger over her lips as we passed Nathan's room. She took the last door on the right, pulling me into the white and blue tiled bathroom, and locked the door behind her. Hands grasped at skin and lips slammed together as we found each other again. She moaned into my mouth, and satisfaction rolled through me, as my hands dipped to cup her ass. I lifted her to sit on the white porcelain of the sink, sending a small brush and some other torturous-looking makeup devices clattering to the ground in the process. She spread her legs to make room for me, as our kisses grew from demanding to frenzied. Lust and need pulsed through me, the sensation pooling in my balls. I flicked a glance at our reflection in the mirror behind her, and excitement pounded through me. She needed to be naked. Now.

My fingers found the bottom hem of her shirt and I broke our kiss just long enough to pull it over her head. Her tits, a perfect handful, covered in delicate white lace, just begged for my mouth, and I couldn't resist the need to lay my mouth on her. I abandoned my quest to see every inch of her bare for just a moment and sucked her nipple through her bra. A fresh wave of desire crashed down on me when her nipple pebbled under my tongue. She was so fucking perfect, with her smooth skin and her body responding to my every touch.

I ditched my own shirt, and her eyes travelled down over my pecs and abs. I stilled, wanting desperately for her to say something. I wasn't weightlifter built, I knew that. But I was long and lean and had the muscles that came from hours of running with

Low every week. Did she like what she saw? I wanted her to be as turned on by me as I was by her. She pushed my waistband down, freeing my straining cock, before letting her gaze travel back up my body. Her eyes lit up as she looked at me. Like I was a fucking Christmas present with her name on it.

I kissed her hard whilst fumbling to find the clasp on her bra, and I pushed the straps down her arms. She moaned again as I cupped her naked breasts, and I pressed my tongue in her mouth to keep her quiet. Nathan's room wasn't *that* far away.

I trailed my hand down her ribcage and over the curve of her hip, delighting in the feel of her. I took my time, my hand gliding over her bare skin, then down over her skirt before I found the knot she'd tied in it. My fingers snuck underneath, trailing up the inside of her thigh, her legs parting even further as I reached the lace that covered her.

I pulled the soaked material to the side, sliding my finger through the wetness I found waiting there for me, and groaned. "So wet," I murmured into her ear. My heart pounded. I wanted that wetness wrapped around my cock. But not yet. Her head dropped back, clunking onto the mirror, and I dropped my mouth to her nipples as I stroked her clit rhythmically. I remembered how she liked to be touched from the first time. I needed to work her, needed to make her scream. Liquid pooled at the tip of my cock, desperate to join the party, and I gave it a quick stroke.

"Fuck, Elodie," I whispered as I leaned in to suck her neck. "I want in."

Her eyes opened, and she pushed me back so she could slide off the sink. Her tits bounced as she moved around the small space, and I ached to have them in my mouth again. She opened the under-sink cupboard and pulled a box of condoms from the very back. She shook it, and with a grin I grabbed it from her before fishing out a foil packet. Elodie threw the box back in its spot and turned to hoist herself back onto the sink, but I grabbed her round the waist.

I had a better idea. I spun her around, so we both faced the mirror.

Elodie's nipples were still wet from my mouth, and her lust-filled eyes stared back at me. I smiled slowly as I positioned her hands on the sink and nudged her thighs apart. She looked back over her shoulder at me, and I shook my head and whispered in her hair. "Watch."

A pink blush broke out over her cheeks, but she did as I'd asked. I kissed a path along her shoulder toward her neck, flicking my tongue over her skin and letting my teeth graze her most sensitive areas.

All while I held her gaze in the mirror.

I hooked my thumbs inside the waistband of her skirt and pulled the skirt and her underwear slowly down her legs, leaving her naked in the reflection. My cock pressed hard into her back and the thought of thrusting deep inside her almost had me losing it right then and there. Her breaths came in soft pants, letting me know she was as turned on as I was by the visual display.

I ripped the top off the condom packet, tossing aside the rubbish and rolling the latex over my cock. I stroked it twice, letting her watch in the mirror, before I moved in behind her again. My palm flattened at the base of her spine and slowly dragged upwards, pushing her upper body down gently.

The blunt head of my cock found her opening, sliding along her wet heat, but I wouldn't press in until I knew she was ready. Instead I leant over her so my chest pressed against her back, and reached around to squeeze her nipple. My other hand sought out her little bundle of nerves and when I found it between her legs, slick and swollen, I rubbed my thumb over it. Over and over I repeated the motions until she moaned loudly. She turned her head again, her mouth seeking mine, her hips jerking.

"I want you inside me," she panted out, a hint of frustration lacing her breath. Her hips pressed back once more, searching for something only I could give her in that moment. And I wanted to give it to her. I wanted to give her everything I'd been thinking about all week. Orgasms and affection. Loyalty. Trust. Everything she'd never gotten from Rick. I lined myself up again, and my cock found home as she sheathed me in one long stroke.

"You're so warm," I mumbled into her neck as I pushed into her, before retreating, then pushing back. My fingers rubbed her centre, and her legs parted even further as she leant over the sink, pushing her ass and hips back. Our eyes met in the mirror as I straightened to pump in and out of her. The green depths of her eyes were hooded yet full of want, and they spurred me on. My pace increased, and she changed her rhythm to match me. A delicious pinkness glowed on her fair skin, her nipples darker and erect. So fucking beautiful. Her eyes closed, head tipped back. I was on the verge of falling into a pleasure abyss and I hoped to God she was too. I wouldn't let go until she did.

"There," she moaned. "Right there." As her walls clenched around me, I fucked her harder. Our thighs slapped in the otherwise quiet bathroom, her orgasm sending me crashing into my own. I rode it out, thrusting slower until her legs trembled.

She leaned hard on the sink, and I braced myself over her, enjoying the shivers coursing through her body. She turned in my arms and pressed her palms to my lower back as my arms circled round her. Her head tilted, and I dropped my mouth to hers, waiting for our heart rates to slow. Long, wet kisses. Open mouthed. Sloppy. I missed her the instant I moved away to pull the condom off and throw it in the bin.

"That was incredible," she whispered when I had her in my arms again.

"The best." My heart pounded, but I wasn't lying. That had been some of the hottest sex I'd ever had. I knew I'd be replaying it in my head for weeks. "I'll turn on the shower for you." I reached for the shower door, but she shook her head and grabbed a towel from the rack beside the bath. "I'm just going to check on Nathan. Though I assume we didn't wake him up since he isn't banging on the door." She gave me a smile. "Plus, the shower is tiny. You go first, and I'll jump in when you're done."

I frowned as she wrapped herself in the towel, hating that she was no longer naked. "One question?"

She stopped, her hand hovering over the doorknob.

"Are there any other rooms in this house that have a lock?"

10

ELODIE

I liked having Jamison in my bed. The sex in the bathroom had been amazing—visual and exciting—but having him in my bed felt...comfortable. We'd climbed beneath the sheets after our showers and found each other in the darkness between giggles and shushing each other to be quiet. As I snuggled against his chest, his fingers had stroked along my bare back, until I'd tipped my chin up to kiss him. I'd lost track of how long we'd kissed for, our mouths moving in unison and our tongues tangling as our fingers explored each other's bodies. Until he'd pushed me back into the mattress, parted my legs, and pushed deep inside me. I'd been more than ready for him. He'd slid in and out of my body, so slowly, every inch a delicious agony. Every cell of my body had screamed for more. But then his eyes had locked with mine in the low light, and there'd been something more than just heat there. Something so overwhelming, I'd stilled in the intensity of it. Suddenly, we weren't just fucking. We were forming a connection. We were making love. The feeling scared me, but even in the short time we'd known each other, I'd come to trust him.

After he'd disposed of the condom, we'd lain together again, my fingers trailing over the ridges of his abs and the rise of his pecs. His lips pressed to my forehead.

"I should go so I'm not here when Nathan wakes up." Jamison's deep timbre was soft in the quiet room. His breaths were slow, and his fingertips combed through my hair, pushing strands away from my face.

"Just stay a bit longer. He'll sleep 'til seven. We'll get up at six and sneak you out."

"Just like being back in high school and sneaking out of my girlfriend's room before her parents woke up."

"Did you really do that?"

He nodded against my head. "Yeah, regularly." He chuckled. "I even knew which of the steps creaked if you stood on the left-hand side, so I always stepped over that one."

"Rick and I never did that. I was too much of a goody two shoes for that sort of thing. I didn't like being in trouble, so I never caused any."

"So, I'm corrupting you then?"

I smiled into his chest. "I guess you are. I really should make you leave. But I like having you here too much."

"Me too. I don't want to leave."

"Then don't."

The silence drew out between us, but it was warm and comfortable. My chest rose and fell in time with his, and my eyes grew heavy. I pressed my lips to his chest once more, before I could fall asleep.

"Elodie?" he murmured.

"Mmm?" I was so thoroughly and delightfully spent, I could barely muster up the energy to respond.

"Do you want to be my girlfriend?"

My eyes flew open and all thoughts of sleep vanished. I lifted my head so I could check to see if he was serious. "Sorry, what?" Butterflies took flight in my stomach and a slightly panicked feeling spread through me. I'd heard what he'd said perfectly, but I needed time to process it.

"Go steady with me. Make this official. Don't date other people. Whatever you want to call it." He trailed his fingers over my collarbone and the swell of my breasts. "I like you."

There was a pure, sweet honesty in his voice, one that went straight to my heart. And for the briefest moment, the word *yes* burned my tongue. I liked him too. More than I'd liked anyone in a very long time. And there was something between us. Something right and comfortable. Something that screamed at me to accept and see where this went. My body wanted him, and I thought maybe a tiny part of my heart did too. But then the logical side of my brain kicked in, throwing up all the reasons I shouldn't. I'd only been single five minutes. I barely knew the man. He was too young; he hadn't even finished Uni. His life would change dramatically when he graduated and he wouldn't want to be tied down to a girlfriend. Especially a girlfriend with as much baggage as I had. What if he got sick of playing happy family and it wasn't only me with a broken heart, but Nathan too? I couldn't be that irresponsible.

I kissed his lips softly. "I can't."

His head dropped back to the pillow and he stared at the ceiling for a long moment, before twisting to kiss my forehead. "Okay."

Disappointment crashed over me, hard and strong, but in my heart, I knew it was the right thing to do. It didn't mean I liked it, though. "I can't make that sort of commitment. It wouldn't be fair to you. Or Nathan."

"It's too early. I get it."

"Exactly. I can't just think of myself. There's Nathan, and Rick…"

The arm beneath my head stiffened. "Rick? What's he got to do with it?"

"He's Nathan's father. He's always going to be in my life."

"Of course. But what has that got to do with us?"

I shook my head. I didn't know. I didn't know why I'd even said Rick's name while I was lying in the arms of a new man. A man I really liked.

"Jamison, I—"

"You know what? It's three a.m. We're both tired. Let's talk about it in the morning."

His voice was gentle, but then he took a deep breath and closed his eyes. I rolled away from him, to my side of the bed. Shit. I didn't want this to end. Not yet. I needed time. I scrambled for a way to fix the situation, but he was right. I was tired and it took me a long time to think of what I wanted to say.

"Jamison? There's a dinner coming up at work, on February 20th. It's at the racecourse actually. It's a really big deal; all the managing partners and our biggest clients will be there." Hope filled my chest. "Will you come with me?" The dinner was still a few weeks away, but I was trying to give him something. Some sign that told him I wanted more than what we'd had so far.

Just say yes. I can't commit to anything long term, but see that I'm trying. Say yes.

He didn't move. His breaths were slow and even, and after a long moment, I sighed and rolled over so my back was to him. I was pretty sure he wasn't asleep.

11

JAMISON

I was already awake when Elodie's alarm went off at six a.m. I hadn't really slept, disappointment sitting heavy on my chest. I hadn't meant to ask Elodie for more last night, but everything had just felt…right. I knew she had a lot of baggage, but I didn't care. I liked her a lot. She was smart and kind and beautiful. And the fact that she was an amazing mother only made her more appealing. Nathan was a great kid, and since Rick was a dick, that awesomeness in him had to have come from Elodie. After we'd fucked like horny teenagers in the bathroom, we'd had slow, soul-connecting sex in her bed. At least I thought we had.

With her lying in my arms afterwards, I'd realised the thought of her dating anyone else was unbearable. I wanted her. And even though things had moved quickly between us, I wanted more. I didn't want to see other women, and I sure as hell didn't want her seeing other men. The words had tumbled from my mouth before I could even really consider the impact of them. But even in the silence that followed, I hadn't wanted to take them back. I'd just wanted her to say yes.

But she hadn't. And my feelings had been hurt, and so I'd

sulked like a preschooler. Fucking dumb ass. Then I'd lain awake for the rest of the night, waiting for her to wake up so I could apologise and beg and grovel for her forgiveness. We could take this as slow as she wanted.

She sat up, the white sheets slipping off her still naked body, exposing her breasts and making my mouth dry. I turned away, already fighting a morning erection, which wasn't helped by the sight of all that creamy skin and her pink nipples. She turned the alarm off and tucked the sheet up around her.

"You'd better go," she said quietly. "Nathan will be awake soon."

Right. That was why she'd set the alarm in the first place. So I could sneak out before Nathan woke up. With heavy limbs, I scooped up my clothes from the floor. I pulled on my shorts slowly, trying to think of what to say to close the gap between us this morning. Every speech I'd rehearsed in my head suddenly seemed stupid. She watched me as I turned my shirt out the right way, and I decided that a simple apology would go down better with her than any of the elaborate rubbish I'd come up with last night.

My fingers bunched in the fabric of my T-shirt as nerves tangled in my gut. I had feelings for her. I'd acknowledged them in the dark of the night and now it was all I could do to keep them to myself. I needed to fix this. "Elodie, I—"

Elodie's head whipped around as three loud thumps came from the front door. She stood, pulling the sheet with her and lifted a blind to peek out the window. She dropped it quickly, and when she turned back to me, her eyes were wide. "It's Rick."

She dropped the sheet, yanking a silky robe from a hanger in her wardrobe, and slipped her arms through before tying it in a knot.

"Are you expecting him?" I asked, just as Rick thumped on the door again.

She shook her head quickly. "No, but he's going to wake up

Nathan if I don't get out there." She glanced at the door and then the window and I wondered if she was trying to work out if I could jump out of it without being seen. "Wait here, okay? I'll come get you when the coast is clear."

I frowned, but this was her show and her rules. Arguing with her wasn't going to get us back to where we'd been last night before I'd opened my big mouth.

The banging came again and Elodie cursed quietly under her breath as she exited the room, leaving me with nothing to do but sit and brood. The house was so quiet and Elodie's room was so close to the front door, I heard every footstep she made along the hallway before she stopped and the sound of turning locks floated back to me.

"What are you doing here?" Elodie hissed at Rick before he could say anything. "And why are you banging my door down? You're going to wake up Nathan!"

I stared at the ceiling, not wanting to eavesdrop, but not really having much choice unless I put my head under a pillow. And after the scene Rick and Bree had created in the restaurant, my protective instincts were on alert. I didn't trust Rick as far as I could throw him. I knew Elodie could handle herself, but I couldn't just tune out.

"Let me in, Elodie. We need to talk." There was a shuffling, and I didn't hear any protests from Elodie, so I assumed she'd done what he asked. The front door closed, but there were no footsteps so I guessed they were still standing in the entry foyer.

"What do you want, Rick? I don't even know why you're here. It's not your day to collect Nathan. Aren't you still supposed to be on your honeymoon?"

"I didn't go. Bree went by herself."

My eyebrows shot up.

"What?" Elodie exclaimed, astonishment in her tone. She sounded as shocked as I was. "Why?"

"I've called it off. The whole thing. The honeymoon. The marriage. All of it. I made a huge mistake."

There was a beat of silence between them and I would have given anything to see the look on Elodie's face.

"Well, that's...I don't even know what that is. I'm sorry?"

I stifled a laugh. Bree and Rick were as fickle as each other. It didn't surprise me their relationship had crumbled so easily. Nothing good came from a relationship that started in a sea of lies and betrayal.

"I made a huge mistake, baby. I never loved her. Not the way I love you. I just got restless and sidetracked and, well, the grass isn't greener on the other side. I know that now."

The smile fell from my face and I pushed to my feet. Anger boiled through me. He had to be kidding. He couldn't possibly think he could come crawling back here after cheating on Elodie and then she'd take him back. We might not have been officially a couple, but there was something between us. We both knew it. I knew Rick had seen it that night at the restaurant. That was probably what had set this into motion. Jealous prick. I paced the length of the room, fighting the urge to storm out there and punch Rick in his dickish face. But I knew Elodie wouldn't appreciate that.

"You've got balls, Rick. I give you that," Elodie said, sounding tired.

I wanted to high-five her.

"You cheat on me, divorce me, marry someone else. Then less than a month later, you want to come back?"

There was more shuffling before Rick's voice came again, pleading this time. "I know, Ellie, I fucked things up royally. I know. But we've been together since we were kids. You're my other half. My soulmate. I don't work right without you. I see that now. I just need one more chance. I can make this up to you and to Nathan. I'll work less, and we can go on a family holiday, just the three of us, like you've been asking me to do for years."

I wanted to gag on the bullshit spewing from his lips, but I didn't hear Elodie's response. She'd lowered her voice, and all I could make out was a murmur. Did she not want me to hear what she was saying? My gut began to churn as a sick feeling swept over me. She wasn't seriously falling for this bullshit, was she? What if she was? What if she still loved him, or thought Nathan would be better off with them together?

Curiosity got the better of me, and even though Elodie had told me to stay put, I padded down the hall on bare feet and poked my head cautiously around the corner. Elodie had her back to me, but Rick's gaze flicked to mine. Surprise and horror washed over Rick's face as I stepped into the foyer and crossed my arms over my chest.

A blur of red and blue pyjamas and messed up blond hair ran past me as if I weren't even there and skidded around the corner. "Daddy!" In a second, Rick's confusion morphed into a calculating smile that made my skin crawl.

Nathan took a running leap at his father and Rick grunted softly as he caught him and lifted him up into his arms. "Hey, buddy!" He ruffled Nathan's hair and kissed his cheek.

"Rick, you should go. We'll talk about this later. Now isn't a good time."

"What?! NO! Daddy, stay! Please!" Nathan yelled.

Elodie reached out and stroked the back of her hand down Nathan's arm. "Daddy can't stay, Nate. This isn't his home anymore. He needs to go back to his place."

"Yes, it is his home!" Nathan wailed, his face scrunching up. "It is! I want him to stay."

Rick used his free hand to cup the side of Elodie's face. He tugged her close and anger burned in my chest as I watched her go without resisting. Her head tilted back as she looked up at him. "It was always you and me, Ellie. We're a family. Let me come home and make it up to you. Can't you see how much it means to Nathan?"

Rick's head lowered until his lips hovered just over Elodie's, but I'd seen enough. I closed the space between the happy family and where I stood as an outsider.

"Jamison!" Elodie gasped. Like she'd forgotten I was even there. Rick's eyes darted to mine and the smugness practically glowed from him. If Nathan hadn't been nestled in his arms with his head on Rick's shoulder, I would have shoved his ugly face into a wall.

I picked up my shoes at the door and reached for the door handle, and Elodie's slim fingers wrapped around my wrist. "Jamison, wait!"

I whirled around, noticing Rick had moved further into the house, standing in the living room doorway like a returning fucking king, home from some battle.

Fuck. Him.

I looked down at Elodie's hand, feeling the disappointment of last night's discussion course though me and mingle with the anger. Had she just been waiting for him to come back this entire time? Is that why she wouldn't make a commitment to me?

I softened my voice. This may not have gone the way I'd wanted it to, but I wasn't going to lower myself to being an asshole about it. "It's fine, Elodie. I get it. You're a family. And he's Nathan's dad."

"But, I—"

I sighed. "Am I wrong?"

Her eyes filled with tears, but she didn't correct me.

"Thought so," I said sadly.

"Wait! Jamison, I—"

Her fingers slipped from my arm as I turned the doorknob and let myself out.

12

ELODIE - TWO WEEKS LATER

*N*athan stood on the side of the lounge and flipped off it, landing on his back amongst the cushions. He scrambled to his feet and did it again. He'd been peering through the window for an hour, waiting for Rick, when I'd suggested he show me his front flips. I hadn't been able to just stand by and watch his growing disappointment as the minutes ticked by and Rick continued to not show up. So I'd resorted to an age-old mum trick. Distraction.

"Mum, when is Jamison coming back? He still has to teach me how to do backflips."

I paused, clutching the shirt I'd been folding. "I'm not sure, mate."

"Can't you call him? He knows how to do all the fun stuff." He bent his knees, poising himself to jump again, when he stopped and peered through the slatted blinds covering the window.

"Dad's here!" Nathan whooped as he jumped off the lounge, landing on the floorboards with the thunk. "And he's brought a truck! Awesome!"

I took a deep breath, willing myself to calm down. Nathan might have instantly forgiven his father for being over an hour late, but I hadn't. Rick hadn't even bothered to call this time. He'd been late two other times this week, but at least then he'd called to apologise. Not that apologies meant much to a little boy being tucked in at night by his mum, when he really wanted his dad. I sighed, trying to calm the adrenaline riling me up for a fight. That wouldn't help anyone.

Nathan jumped at the deadlock on the back of the door, but he was too short to even touch it, let alone turn it.

"Hold up, Nate." I put down the washing I'd been folding. "I'll get it."

I wasn't even three steps toward the door when the lock turned and the door swung in. Nathan jumped out of the way before it collected him. "Dad!"

I frowned as Nathan launched himself at Rick's legs. "How did you get in? Did I leave my keys in the lock?"

"I took the spare and made myself a new copy." He held up the two keys dangling on a simple ring like they were a medal. Irritation made the back of my neck prickle. I had no idea why he looked so proud of himself.

"You could have asked." My eyebrows pulled together.

"That would have ruined my surprise."

I folded my arms across my chest, a sense of dread coming over me. I didn't think I was going to like where this was heading. "What surprise is that?"

He pushed the front door open further, pointing back to the street. "I hired a truck!" Nathan ran past him and sprinted across the grass to where a solidly built man was opening the back of the large vehicle.

"Who's that?"

"His name is Tony. He's the maintenance man at the firm. I hired him for a few hours to help me move."

My stomach sank. "Move…" But Rick was already following Nathan back out to the road. I trailed behind them, dread gnawing at my gut. Tony unlocked the back of the truck and disappeared inside, reappearing a moment later with Rick's favourite reading lamp, the one that had always stood by his office desk. My mouth gaped open as I took in a truck full of furniture—the furniture he'd moved out of the house just a few months earlier.

"You're moving back in?!" Nathan squealed.

Rick scooped him up and lifted him to his shoulder, before holding up his palm for a high five. Nathan slapped it, grinning from ear to ear.

"Sure am, buddy." He glanced over at me. "If that's okay with Mummy, of course?" He gave me a smile that was probably supposed to be boyishly charming. I'd always loved that smile when we were teenagers, but suddenly it looked poisonous and manipulative.

One by one, I uncurled each of my fingers from the fists I'd formed without even noticing. I gave Nathan the brightest smile I could muster.

"Boss, where do you want this?" Tony asked, holding up a canvas covered in brightly coloured swirls of paint. It was a painting Rick's mother had done years earlier and I'd always hated it.

"It goes in the foyer," Rick answered.

Like hell it did. I'd chosen a beautiful watercolour the day after Rick left that had filled that spot in the foyer ever since. No way was I giving that up without even a word. But I didn't want to argue in front of Tony. Or in front of Nathan. So instead I sucked in a deep breath of air, slowly filling my lungs completely, before letting it out in an equally slow puff. Rick shot me a questioning look, which I ignored. I couldn't believe he thought he could just move his stuff back in without so much as a conversation. He knew how that conversation would have gone—I might have broken up with Jamison, but I hadn't made any commitments to Rick. I'd allowed him to come for dinner, twice of which he'd blown off to stay back at work. But I'd been trying, because having Rick around more meant the world to Nathan. And Nathan's happiness meant the world to me.

Nathan had come home with an award for good behaviour on Friday afternoon, which just proved to me I was doing the right thing by allowing Rick to be around more. But my heart wasn't in it. I missed Jamison. I missed his goofy, sarcastic jokes, and the magnetised pull I felt whenever he was around. It was a stark contrast to the way I was avoiding Rick's touch. I'd been trying for two weeks now to bottle up everything I felt for Jamison, to shove a cork in it and bury it in the sand that had become my heart. But I still wasn't any closer than when he'd walked out my front door.

"Nate, do you want to go get a chocolate milkshake at Dream Bean?" Dream Bean was a local coffee shop Nathan and I went to regularly. I needed to get out of this house. I couldn't watch Rick move his junk back in for a minute longer without wanting to throw it all through a window.

"Great idea. I'll come too. I'd kill for a caramel cappuccino," Rick answered before Nathan could even open his mouth.

"Don't you need to stay here and help Tony?" The edge of frost that touched my words surprised me. I wasn't one to start a confrontation, but Rick didn't comment on it, if he even noticed.

"Nah, he's got this." He slapped the bigger man on the back and patted his back pocket. "I've got my wallet. Let's go."

It was a short ten-minute walk to the Dream Bean, and Nathan filled the air with his little boy chatter, excited to have his dad after waiting for him half the afternoon. The exercise and fresh air improved my mood, and by the time we reached the store, I'd vowed to put my negative feelings about Rick moving back in behind me.

We ordered our drinks at the counter and chose a huge piece of black forest cake to share. Rick led us to a small, white table in the centre of the room and we sat down around it. Nathan's little feet dangled off the edge of his chair.

Rick sat back, crossing his legs at the ankle, generally taking up more room than he really needed to. A slow smile spread across his face. "So, I have a surprise for the two of you."

"Is it a puppy?!" Nathan asked, glancing beneath the table. I couldn't help but laugh at how cute he was.

"Daddy doesn't have a puppy hidden under there, mate," I said gently. Nathan pouted.

"No, I don't. But maybe when we get back from Canada we can get one!"

My mouth dropped open. I had no words. My brain completely blanked, as I tried to make sense of Rick's statement.

"What?" I choked.

"Do you know where Canada is, Nate? It's really cold there right now, not hot like it is here in Sydney. I know your mum has always wanted to go, so I booked tickets for us. We leave next week."

"I get to go on an aeroplane? Or do we have to drive?"

Rick chuckled. "Definitely going on a plane, little guy. Canada is on the other side of the world to Australia."

"Yes! I want a window seat, and can I…"

Nathan's excited chatter washed over me. "Rick, are you serious?" The unmistakable purple colour of the Lavender Fields Racecourse uniforms caught my eye from the registers. My heart thumped inside my chest before I realised it wasn't Jamison standing there. The petite frame and long, dark hair were familiar, though, and Reese raised a hand in a tentative wave. Great. Seeing Reese while I was out with Rick was only marginally better than seeing Jamison. She'd go straight back to work and tell him, no doubt.

"You wanted me to spend more time with you, so that's what I'm doing."

My eyes trailed Reese and she sat at a table just a few meters away to my right. I leant forward and lowered my voice to a whisper. "I meant I wanted you to come home for dinner on time, maybe have family Sundays. Not go on a trip to Canada!"

"Go big or go home, El."

"Don't call me that," I snapped before I even thought about it.

Rick huffed. "Come on, Elodie. You've always wanted to go skiing, and we can do some sightseeing."

"Rick! We can't! I have work, and Nathan has school! He's been in enough trouble as it is; he can't be just missing class on top of it all! What message does that send? Get detention at school and we'll take you on holiday?"

Rick's eyes darkened. "I've already booked the tickets. We're going."

I gaped at him. Since when did he think he could dictate my life? Since when did he even have a say in it? Anger surged through me and I jammed my arms across my chest. "No, we're not."

I sat back in my chair, as Rick's face turned an unsightly combination of red and purple. My eye caught on Reese, who was unashamedly staring.

Are you okay? she mouthed, her pretty features strained in concern.

Dammit. I didn't want Reese to see this. I didn't want anyone in this coffee shop to see this. I nodded curtly to Reese and grabbed Rick's hand. "We need to leave."

Rick pushed to his feet and Nathan followed the two of us quietly. I felt Reese's concerned gaze follow me until we were out of sight.

13

JAMISON

*L*ow blew out a long breath as he leant back on the dishwasher. "Really, Jam? You wait until my very last shift to ask me to cover for you on the weekend? Your timing sucks, mate."

I rolled my eyes. "You're only moving out to the stables. It's not like you're leaving the company. One extra shift won't kill you." I eyed him. "Plus, you said yourself, you owe me after all the shit you and Reese pulled last year. I covered for both your asses multiple times. Remember?"

A hint of guilt flashed in Low's eyes and he dropped his arms. He ran his hand through his hair, leaving it resting on the back of his neck. "Fair enough. I'll cover the function for you. I still think you should do it though. You need to get her out of your system."

I shook my head. "I can't. I get why she chose him, but I don't want to see them together, parading around like some happy family when I know what a scumbag he is."

"Maybe he's changed. People do."

"Not him."

Low frowned. "She really got under your skin, didn't she?

That was the understatement of the century.

"You've done nothing but mope and talk about her for weeks. I've never seen you so hung up on someone."

I huffed and ran a cloth over a splodge of water on the bar top. I didn't bother answering. I couldn't deny it. My logical brain understood why Elodie had chosen to go back to Rick, and I respected her decision. But *fuck*. It made me feel hollow inside. I'd been falling for her, and having it yanked away before we really had the chance to explore it made my chest ache. I was plagued with thoughts of her. While I was running, I thought about how easy it was to talk to her. While I was working, I thought about how kind and good she was. While I was studying, I thought about the curve of her hip and the sway of her ass. And then I'd have to go take a cold shower to relieve my frustrations. My body kept moving, but my heart was elsewhere. And as much as I didn't want to admit it, I was sad and disappointed.

"Jamison." The feminine voice startled me from my thoughts. If I'd had my wits about me, I probably would have recognised Bree's brassy tones and run in the other direction. Funny how one voice can sound completely sexy one day, but then sound like cats on a hot tin roof the next.

I caught the scowl on Low's face before I answered. "What are you doing here, Bree?"

She tapped her long, red nails on the bar top, the sound instantly grating on my nerves. "Do you get a lunch break?"

"No."

Low snorted and turned away.

She gave me an overstated pout that she probably thought was sexy but just looked ridiculous on a grown woman. "Please?"

"Fine." I glanced over at Low. "Cover for ten minutes?"

"You got it."

I pushed open the bar door and walked a few feet away to a vacant table. Bree followed, sitting herself in the chair next to me instead of across from me. "What's up?"

"Rick left me."

"I know."

"He's back with his princess, isn't he?"

That was rich coming from her. Elodie was as far removed from a princess as Bree was removed from down to earth. "Jealousy doesn't look good on you, Bree."

"It didn't look good on you at the wedding either," she snipped.

"Did you think I was jealous?"

"Isn't that why you made such a scene?"

I thought back over the night I'd met Elodie, and all I could remember was losing myself in her eyes and being hung up on every word she said. I just remembered having fun. Laughing. Feeling that spark of connection and attraction that made you want to do dumb things. Like kiss a woman you barely knew on stage while singing "Love Shack." A grin pulled at my mouth.

"Jamison! Are you even listening to me?"

"What?"

"Rick. He won't take my calls, but I know Elodie's company is having a big bash here next weekend. Can you get me in?"

"What's wrong with you? They have a kid together, Bree. Doesn't a family being together mean anything to you?"

She laughed, the sound cruel and uncaring. "Rick didn't care too much about that when he was relentlessly pursuing me. I tried to keep him at bay because I was with you, but..."

"But you just couldn't help yourself," I said dryly.

She shrugged. "You couldn't give me what I wanted."

"Thank God for that," I muttered under my breath. My blood boiled all over again at the thought of Elodie and Nathan at home alone while Rick was out chasing other men's girlfriends. What a charmer he was. Bree and him, both.

"I think we're done here."

"What? No! Are you going to get me into the party? We could go together." A calculating light shone in her eyes. "Rick'd hate seeing me saunter in on your arm. That's why he's back with her, you know? He couldn't stand seeing the two of you all over each other."

I stared at her, bewildered. I didn't even recognise her. Was she this mean and vindictive when we'd been dating?

"What's gotten into you? Why are you being like this?"

She tapped her talons on the form guide someone had left on the table. "Like what?"

I scoffed. "You've been downright cruel to Elodie. And you've treated me like shit. You've never been easy to handle, but you were never this vicious either. What's changed?"

She bristled, her eyes blazing fire. But I waited, refusing to look away, safe in the knowledge her words held no truth. Elodie and I had already apologised for making a scene at the wedding. We hadn't done anything else to deserve Bree's wrath. And I deserved an explanation.

I watched the fire in Bree's eyes die, only to be replaced by tears.

Shit.

"Hey," I said, softening my tone. "Don't cry." I glanced over at Low who was watching from the bar and gave him a panicked look. I didn't know what to do with a crying Bree. This was uncharted territory. He shrugged and scuttled away into the kitchen. Asshole. Fat lot of help he was.

Bree shook her head and blinked hard, but it did little to help. A choked sob rose from her chest and my eyes widened.

"Shit, Bree. I'm sorry. Please stop." I patted her hand awkwardly, wishing I'd never called her on her bullshit. I'd never seen her cry before. She had always been tough as nails. I hadn't realised she was capable of emotion.

Her bottom lip trembled and in that moment, I saw her. Real. Honest. Raw. For the first time ever, I saw beneath the makeup and the attitude and the walls she put up to keep everyone at bay. "Everyone always leaves me," she said miserably. A tear tracked down her cheek. "Rick. My sister. My ex. All I ever wanted was for someone to love me for who I am. For them to stay."

I swallowed hard and cleared my throat. I knew it couldn't have been easy for her to lay her skeletons on the table like that. But at the same time...

"You cheated on me, Bree. Did you forget that? You were the one that pushed me away, not the other way around."

She pulled her purse onto her lap and clutched it tightly. "You were never really there, though. Physically, sure. But I knew you were never going to love me. I knew your feelings didn't run that deep."

"Neither did yours."

"They might have."

I gave her a disbelieving look, and the corner of her mouth lifted.

"Fine. I didn't feel like that either. But that's why I let Rick pursue me. It felt nice to be truly wanted by someone. And then he left his wife and proposed... I thought he was the real deal. But then he was so jealous over you and Elodie hooking up..." She sniffed and let her blond hair fall around her face. "He was just the same as Timothy."

"Timothy?"

She nodded. "High-school boyfriend turned brother-in-law. Remember?"

I remembered. I wasn't surprised that being dumped by Rick brought up old memories for her. "I don't know what to tell you, Bree. Guys like Timothy and Rick? They're weak. And in the end, they're the ones that miss out. Don't follow them down that road. Do something about your anger issues, and let the next guy see the real you. I know there's a good person hidden behind all your walls and spikes and armour. One day, some guy is going to smash through it all, if you let him. I want that for you, Bree. I truly do. That guy is worth waiting for."

She gave me a wobbly smile. But it was an honest one and

made her look years younger. "Thank you. That was kind. And I know I don't deserve it." She paused before adding, "You're a good guy, Jamison."

I shrugged. "Don't tell anyone."

We both rose to our feet and she kissed me quickly on the cheek before heading to the exit. I watched as she opened the glass doors and almost collided with Reese who was coming in from outside. Bree disappeared into the crowd as I stood next to Low, who'd obviously thought it safe enough to reappear now that the crying had stopped.

"Jamison!" Reese called as she hurried over, breathing heavily, her cheeks flushed pink. Low intercepted her, catching her by the shoulders, his worried gaze searching her face. "Hey, what's wrong?"

Reese gave him a quick smile. "Nothing, I'm fine. I just need to talk to Jam."

"Okay, then." He dropped a kiss on her head and moved aside to let her by.

"What's up?" I asked when she stopped in front of me, her chest rising and falling rapidly. I eyed her empty hands. "Where's the coffee?"

She looked blankly at me. "Shit, sorry. I completely forgot."

I laughed. "So, what did you do at the coffee shop then?"

"That's what I'm trying to tell you, if the two of you would just let me get a word in."

Low and I both stood obediently silent and waited.

"I saw Elodie at the coffee shop."

My heart sunk.

"She was with Rick and Nathan."

I stacked a pile of coasters on the bench top, shuffling them so they all lined up neatly. "Not exactly helpful info for me right now, Reese. But thanks for the neighbourhood watch report."

"Just shut up and listen, will you? Something isn't right there.

She didn't look happy at all. And neither did Nathan. Elodie and Rick spent the whole time I was there arguing."

I frowned. "Couples fight."

"Not like this. I think you should call her."

"She won't want to speak to me."

She slapped the back of her hand across my chest. "What, you can't call and check in with a friend? She looked like she could use one."

My heart rate picked up and a question lodged in my throat. "You...you don't think Rick is hurting her, do you?"

Relief calmed my pulse when Reese shook her head vigorously. "No, she looked in control of the situation. Nothing made me think she was in physical danger. But she just looked miserable. I wanted to talk to her, but she rushed out of the shop pretty much as soon as she saw me."

I mulled it over. I couldn't just call or go over. I'd promised myself I'd leave her alone, let them have a chance at being a family again. But damn if every nerve ending in my body wasn't urging me to go straight there and make sure she and Nathan were okay.

"Low? I'm going to need my Saturday night shift in the function room back."

14

ELODIE

I didn't bother knocking on the rust-covered screen door, just pulled it open and let myself in. The familiar smell of my mother's spaghetti sauce greeted me as I made my way down the hall to the kitchen.

"Mum?" I called, when I found the brightly coloured kitchen empty. My mother loved bright colours, so when she'd remodelled the house about ten years back, she'd put in a bright red backsplash and countertop, with black cupboards. She'd decorated with pops of yellow. The result was somewhat blinding, to my more conservative taste, but it was uniquely her. And it was home. I eyed the bubbling pot on the stove, picking up the wooden spoon resting on the bench to give it a quick stir. I'd learnt to make spaghetti sauce right here in this kitchen, standing on a chair so I could stir and add ingredients to the sauce. The back door swung open, and my mother appeared with a handful of basil leaves. Her permed hair was piled onto the top of her head and held in place with a clip. She jumped when she saw me, her hand covering her heart. "Oh Lord, Elodie. Don't sneak up on an old woman like that."

I rolled my eyes and kissed her on the cheek. "You're not old and you know it." She'd only turned fifty last month.

"Well, if you keep sneaking in here like that, you'll age me prematurely." She looked over my shoulder into the living room. "Where's Nate?"

"With Rick."

"Oh." My mother did nothing to hide her disappointment.

I laughed. "Sorry. I promise I'll bring him over for you to spoil during the week."

She rinsed the basil leaves under the tap, before handing them to me to rip and throw into the sauce. Even though I wasn't looking at her, I could feel her studying me.

"What, Mum?"

"Nothing."

I turned to her and gave her a look. "Spill it."

She sighed. "You're a grown woman. You're entitled to make your own decisions. But I think you're making a bad one with Rick."

I added stock to the sauce instead of answering.

"Do you even love him?"

"He's the father of my child."

"Sure, you love him as Nathan's dad. But do you, as a woman, love him? Because I haven't seen that sort of love between the two of you since you were kids."

I shook my head. "You didn't see Nate's face when Rick came home. You didn't see how sad he was when he left."

"I see it. But *you're* my child, Elodie. And I see you too. You aren't happy when he's here."

She took the sauce from the stovetop and turned the knob off before she turned back to face me. Without the distraction of the spaghetti, I had nowhere to look except directly into her eyes.

"Why did you take him back? He never makes you his priority. And he's never been as committed to you as you are to him."

I looked to the ceiling. "Thanks, Mum. Good to know you've always thought me pathetic."

She shook her head. "That's a failing on him, not you. It's not a bad thing to love someone with all your heart. But can you really say you still feel the same way?"

Did I really have to go over this again? "Nathan's been so much better at school since Rick's been home. He got a merit award for having a good attitude at his assembly the other day. And Rick says he wants to be here. He wants to change."

"But what do you want? Don't overthink it. Just say it."

"Mum! I don't want to do this right now. We're back together and that's it."

"What do you want, Elodie? Just say it." Her calm tone infuriated me further.

"Stop!"

"What. Do. You. Want?"

My frustration burst its dam and the words exploded from my mouth. "I want Rick to have loved me and Nathan enough to not fucking cheat on me! Is that too much to ask?" My fingers clenched into fists.

"No, it's not. So, what do you want?"

"I want Nathan to be happy."

"He will be. When you are. What else?"

Goddamn it. "Jamison."

Mum paused in her interrogation and lifted an eyebrow. "Jamison?"

Shit. I shouldn't have said that. I looked away until Mum's hand rested on my shoulder. "You don't always have to be perfect, you know?"

I scoffed and threw my hands up in the air. "My husband cheated on me. Married someone else. My kid is miserable. And I ran off the guy I have actual feelings for. I'd hardly call this perfect."

"You've always had an obsession with perfect, Elodie. People always commented on how perfectly well behaved you were as a kid. I could never put that down to my parenting; you just liked being good. You're always polite and kind. You always had perfect grades at school. You married your high-school sweet-heart—the class valedictorian—before you'd even had a single argument." She sighed. "Don't get me wrong. I love that you have such a big heart, and it's an asset to you. But perfect is an illusion, and I think you're beginning to see that."

"Rick will always be his dad."

"Of course. The three of you will always be family. But that doesn't mean you can't make room for someone else. Someone that makes you happy, as well as Nathan."

"It's not that simple, Mum." But a voice inside me, one I'd tried to silence for weeks now, whispered that maybe it was. My brain whirled. There was Jamison coaxing Nathan out of his shell within minutes of meeting him. Nathan's laughter as Jamison slung him over his shoulder and raced toward the jumping castles. His disappointment when Rick hadn't shown up, and the way he'd asked when Jamison was coming back. And one that had been playing on my heart—Nathan's scared, timid face as he'd sat silently between Rick and me as we argued at the coffee shop.

"It can be. If you let it," Mum said gently, before she kissed my cheek and went back to her spaghetti sauce.

15

JAMISON

I'd never seen the function room at the racetrack look so fancy. The walls had been draped in sparkling gold cloth that hung from the high ceilings all the way to the floor. Thousands of fairy lights were strung across the roof, the main lights dimmed to show them off to their full effect. Waiters in crisp white shirts and black ties circled the room with canapes, offering them to the formally dressed partygoers. The men wore black suits, cufflinks glinting at their wrists. Many of the women had gone with shorter, cocktail-length dresses, but there were some full-length skirts in the crowd as well, giving the room an extra elegant feel. Classical music floated over the air, mingling with the many conversations taking place around the space.

Working at a different bar with a different crew of people was strange. I knew from other times I'd picked up these extra shifts that the night would probably drag as we tried to feel our way around each other. We'd only been working for half an hour, but I already felt like I'd been in this over-decorated room for days.

A blond waitress, whose name I couldn't remember, placed her empty tray down on the bar top while she waited for me to refill it with drinks. I mindlessly poured the glasses of champagne, vaguely registering her friendly chatter, but unable to concentrate long enough to take part in it. My gaze kept wandering to the big double doors that opened every few minutes to admit new couples dressed to the nines.

I searched the faces of every new person with a mixture of hope and dread sitting on my chest. Each time I wanted to see Elodie's moss green eyes, while at the same time, part of me hoped she wouldn't come.

Cool liquid cascaded over my hand and I swore, looking down to find I'd overfilled a champagne flute to the point that I'd created a waterfall over the edges. Shaking my head, I tipped the glass toward the sink, then wiped down the outside with some paper towels before I placed it on the tray. The woman gave me a quizzical look but didn't say anything as she moved away with her tray held high above her head.

I mopped up the puddle of champagne I'd made on the bar top and gave myself a kick up the ass. I was working, and I didn't think these people with their fancy clothes and presumably huge salaries would take kindly to a bartender who was fucking things up.

"Jamison."

My heart stopped. I lifted my eyes and my mouth dried at the sight of her. Her hair was swept back in an elegant twist, showing off her long neck and creamy white skin. Her shoulders were bare, the satin of her dress dipping low between her breasts, showing off her cleavage to full effect. The deep-red material swirled across her torso before flaring to a full-length skirt. My palms suddenly felt sweaty, and I tucked them inside my pants. She looked like fucking royalty.

"Wow." I didn't even try to hide the lust I knew burned in my gaze. I couldn't stop looking at her. I drank in every curve of her body and committed each one to memory.

"I just..." She bit her lip before glancing over her shoulder. When she turned back, she took a step closer, resting perfectly polished fingertips on the bar top. Elodie's were simple and elegant though—clear polish with white at the tips. Nothing like the red talons Bree had been sporting when I'd seen her earlier in the week.

Elodie's teeth worried her bottom lip, and I wanted to reach out and run my finger over the pretty pink plumpness of them. "I just wanted to come and say hello, so things aren't weird tonight. I wasn't even sure you'd be working."

I took a deep breath, trying to find some control over my body. "The money is good. I couldn't turn it down."

Her gaze searched my face for a moment too long before she nodded. We both knew my answer was bullshit. There was more to me taking the shift than just the extra coin. "How's Nathan?"

A strange look I couldn't place passed over her features before she forced a smile. "He's good. He loves having his dad home."

I bit the inside of my cheek for a long moment before I replied. "And you? Are you glad to have him home? Reese said…"

Something flickered in Elodie's eyes that made my heart thump triple time. But then she forced a smile, though I saw the tinge of sadness in it. "I guess—"

"There you are!" Rick's booming voice announced as he sauntered to Elodie's side and wrapped his arm around her middle, pulling her close. He gave me a smug grin. My molars ground together. He was all show and no class. Elodie squirmed in his arms, creating distance between them and cementing the idea that maybe everything wasn't as rosy as it seemed. My eyes flicked to hers and she shook her head slightly.

What did that mean?

"What's the CEO's name again, El? John? James? I can never remember," he asked her, his eyes travelling over and resting on a group of men at the front of the room. "They'd be a huge coup for my firm if I could bring them in."

"Rick, I don't think that's a good idea tonight. This isn't supposed to be a business meeting. It's a fundraiser. The man only lost his wife a few months back; he isn't going to want to talk legal representation."

Rick waved his hand around, dismissing her concerns. "I get men like him. Every event is an opportunity for a business meeting." He jerked his head in my direction. "The waiter can bring your champagne over, can't you?" He directed his question to me with all the sweetness of a cobra. "And a bourbon and coke for me."

I nodded, almost rolling my eyes at the predictable way he spoke to me. He might have had all the money in the world, but he was a little man, trying to make himself feel big by putting me down. I couldn't have cared less. Bringing drinks to their group meant more chances to be near Elodie. "Happy to."

Elodie shot me an apologetic look as Rick dragged her off to a group of three men who stood drinking bourbon at the front of the room. I poured their drinks slowly before putting them on a tray. I wiped my hands on a cloth, then rounded the end of the bar and made my way over to their small group. I cleared my throat as I arrived. "Sir?" I said to Rick with a smile that I was sure gave away every ounce of distaste I had for the man. He took his bourbon without so much as looking at me, let alone saying thank you, and I turned my attention to Elodie. I handed her a glass of red wine and said quietly, "I hope you don't mind. I know you don't like champagne."

I hadn't meant for Rick to hear, but his head snapped around. "Of course she does."

She took a tiny step back from him. "No actually, Rick, I don't. I never have."

I wondered if I looked as smug as Rick had earlier. Rick huffed and went back to the conversation. Elodie took a sip of her drink and shot me a tiny smile. I winked at her and turned to walk away but an older woman came barrelling up, almost running straight into me. I stepped to the side, trying to navigate around the crowd of people, but brushed Elodie's arm in the process. The older woman was heavyset; a black shawl draped across her arms and a ruby—so big it had to be costume jewellery —sat centre stage at her throat.

"Elodie, love!" she called loudly, pulling Elodie into her arms and kissing the air somewhere to the side of her face. She turned to Rick and did the same thing. "Rick!" She pulled back, holding him at arm's-length. Her gaze bounced between the two of them, her painted-on eyebrows rising sky high. "Aren't you a sight for sore eyes! I heard the two of you broke up and you married someone else!" I slowed my pace, wanting to tell the old gossip to mind her business.

Rick laughed. The fake sound grated through my nerves. "El here couldn't stay away from me and begged me to come home."

He and the woman laughed loudly as my blood boiled. Before I could stop myself, I dropped the tray with a clatter and spun back, taking three quick steps to close the gap between Rick and myself. My fists clenched. I was really going to enjoy punching him in the face. He'd had it coming for a long time, and Nathan's dad or not, he deserved it.

But before I could even lift an arm, a swirl of red stepped in front of me and slapped Rick square across the jaw. The smack of flesh against flesh rang out, causing the people around us to stop and stare, their mouths hanging open. They weren't the only ones. I stood behind Elodie and gaped at her back. Her body trembled, one hand clenched into a fist, the other shook violently, her palm already pinkening. Holy shit.

"How dare you?" she seethed, seemingly forgetting we were in a room filled with her work colleagues, most of whom were now staring. "You cheat on me, marry someone else, grovel your way back into my life when I was doing just fine without you, and now this? You self-important asshole."

"Elodie," Rick whispered, a fake smile forced across his face. "Stop. People are—"

"No, you stop, Rick. I'm done with this. I wanted it to work—

for Nathan. Because he loves you. And because I had some stupid idea in my head that I needed to keep up the perfect couple with a perfect family facade. But the truth is, we've never been perfect. And I don't want this anymore. We're over."

Rick's face darkened as he rubbed his jaw. "You're making a scene!" he hissed.

She glanced around and gritted her teeth. "You're right. Let's take this outside."

Rick gave a forced smile to the CEO and the old gossip before turning and storming away to the doors. Elodie sighed, the fight going out of her, as she turned to follow him. She stopped when she saw me standing behind her, surprise and embarrassment clouding her eyes. I'm pretty sure my mouth was hanging open. But through my surprise, hope rose. Had she really just broken up with him? Did that mean there was a chance for a future between us?

"You heard all that, huh?"

"Most of the room did. Do you need ice for your hand?"

She shook her head. "I need to go sort this out."

Any hope that had risen in me was put out in an instant. Had I really thought she'd just gasp and fall into my arms? I wasn't her first priority here. As much as it grated at me, she was still running to him. I swallowed hard before I could speak. "I'll get out of your way."

She nodded, giving me one last lingering look, before she sighed and pushed her way through the double doors and out of my sight.

ELODIE

"What the fuck was that!" Rick roared when I eventually found him in the parking lot. He paced up and down in the dim light beside his BMW. I folded my arms across my chest and let him say his piece. "You humiliated me in front of everyone! And not just me, you humiliated yourself."

"Actually, Rick, I humiliated myself when I let you weasel your way back into my life when it wasn't what I wanted. I let you bully me into it, and that was weak. But you knew Nathan was my weak spot and you manipulated me. And I was stupid enough to let you. But, that?" I pointed back to the function room. "Whatever that was you pulled in there? Acting like you're the big man in front of Jamison and my boss? That was the last straw. You don't respect me, and that's not something I want my son to grow up witnessing. We're done."

Rick's posture softened as he stopped pacing. "Look, I'm sorry. I've had too much to drink. We'll talk about this in the morning. Let's go."

"No."

"No?"

"That's what I said. Hear the words coming from my mouth, Rick. We're finished. We'll co-parent, but anything romantic between us is in the past. You should go back to Bree. Or move on with someone else. I don't care. But I mean it when I say, we are never getting back together."

Rick's face was a mess of bewilderment. He threw his hands up in the air. "For fuck's sake, Elodie, whatever." He pulled his keys out of his pocket and I snatched them from his hand quickly.

"What now?!"

"You're not driving home like this. There's a cab rank at the end of the parking lot."

"I'm fine to drive."

"You're not. You may have acted like a complete and utter ass tonight, but you're still Nathan's father and I'm not letting you drive. Walk, Uber, or taxi. They're your choices."

He studied me for a long moment. "You're a bitch when you're like this."

His words stung for a moment. I'd never been called a name like that in my life, but then I remembered who it was coming from and the state he was in.

"Maybe so. Or maybe this is just me standing up and putting myself first. Finally. It's something I should have done a long time ago. And in the morning, you'll see this was me looking out for you too, even though you don't deserve it."

"Whatever. Go back to your waiter, then." He skulked across the parking lot to the road, where a line of taxis sat waiting. He opened the door of the nearest one and disappeared inside, the taxi melting out of sight in the darkness.

My shoulders slumped and I walked back toward the function room slowly, finding a park bench a few metres off the path. I sunk onto it and tilted my head back to take in the night sky. My lungs heaved with the effort of sucking in deep gulps of clean, fresh air. My heart pounded in my chest, slowly coming back to a normal pace now that I didn't have adrenaline coursing through me. I barely recognised my actions in the past hour. Slapping someone in a roomful of people? That was certainly something I'd never had on my bucket list.

Time ticked on as I sat there contemplating the mess that was my life. People started to leave the event, making their way back to their cars and the taxis, but I couldn't find it in me to move. Exhaustion rolled over me, and I gave into it for a moment, closing my eyes. I'd have to talk to Rick in the morning and organise removalists to move him out of the house. We'd need to work out a permanent custody arrangement for Nathan too. None of this half-hearted stuff and just playing it by ear like we had in the past. I was done. We were done.

At least we didn't have to get divorced again. I let out a little laugh of irony, and a smile crept across my face.

The music from inside the function room stopped, the lights coming on, and the rest of the room emptied out. Maybe people didn't see me, sitting over in the darkness, or maybe they did and just didn't want to talk to the woman who had slapped and dumped her ex-husband in the middle of a work function. But either way, nobody spoke to me. I wasn't looking forward to the questions I'd face at work on Monday. That would no doubt be embarrassing. But the relief of not being shackled to Rick for another night made those thoughts a little easier to bear.

I waited until the crowd trickled down to the last few people before I pushed to my feet and made my way back to the function room, in search of my bag. The room was quieter when I pushed through the doors. The fairy lights had been turned off and the wait staff and the DJ were all sitting around a table with beers. They all looked over when I entered, but Jamison's eyes were the ones I sought out. He stood and put down his beer bottle. He took a few steps toward me and held up my clutch bag. "Looking for this?" he asked gently.

I took it from him. My fingers trembled as I tilted my head back to look up. Even though I was in heels, he towered over me.

"Thanks for having my back."

"Anytime."

I dropped my gaze to my fingers and wove them between the strap of the bag. It would be easier to get this out if I didn't have to look him in the eye. "Can we talk?"

His hand dropped to the small of my back and he steered me away from the others who were talking and laughing quietly. He pulled a chair out for me, but I shook my head, preferring to stand, so he perched on the edge of the table instead, which evened out our heights a little. He watched me pace back and forth for a moment before he spoke.

"Elodie, I—"

I grabbed his hand and squeezed it. "No, please. Let me speak first."

"Okay."

"I'm not perfect."

Jamison reached out and tucked a strand of hair behind my ear. "No one is, El."

"Yeah, but it's come to my realisation that I try too hard. And in the process of trying too hard, I managed to lose myself."

"What do you mean?"

I sighed. "I don't know. My mother pointed out that I always put Nathan and Rick before myself. I'm not sure that's entirely true, but trying to fix things just to keep the two of them happy wasn't making me happy." I flexed and unflexed my fingers before I whispered. "That feels incredibly selfish, though."

His fingers trailed up my arm and over my shoulder until his palm cupped my cheek. "It's not."

"I just want things to go back to being easy. And the last time things felt easy was when I was with you." I cleared my throat and straightened my shoulders. I knew he needed to have it laid out, so there was no confusion between us. "I broke up with Rick. We weren't ever really back together though. Not in my mind, anyway."

Jamison pushed to his feet, his fingers sliding into my hair as I tilted my head to look up at him. He dipped his mouth down to hover just over mine, and hope made my heart flutter. "Do you still want to be my boyfriend?" I whispered, butterflies swirling in my stomach like I was fifteen again.

He let out a little chuckle. "What do you think?"

His mouth met mine, and sparks exploded as brightly as if fireworks had gone off around us. Our lips moved in unison, as if we hadn't been apart a minute, let alone a few weeks. Somewhere, part of my brain registered the whistles and catcalls from the other bartenders, and a song filling the air around us, but all I focused on was him. I lost myself in the feel of his lips as his tongue pressed along the seam of my mouth and I opened to him eagerly.

Our tongues moved together, exploring and remembering where we'd last left off. The pressure of his hands—one at the back of my neck, one on my hip, both urging me closer to him. Sparks of hope and happiness rose up in me. He'd seen my imperfections—both the physical and mental ones—and he'd accepted them without hesitation.

I pulled away, breathless, before I jumped him right here in front of everyone. I didn't need to make another scene in this room tonight. It was only then, with a little space from the heady way he made me feel that I realised the song playing was "Love Shack" by the B-52's. The same song we'd sung at the wedding when we first hooked up. I raised an eyebrow. "Did you orchestrate this with the DJ?"

He held his hands up in mock surrender and shook his head, but the glint of mischief in his eyes made me doubt his truthfulness.

"Want to dance?"

I shook my head. "Does this mean "Love Shack is our song now?" I screwed up my nose. "It's not exactly romantic."

His lips pressed against the sensitive spot beneath my ear, making a shiver run down my spine.

"Nothing's perfect."

EPILOGUE

ELODIE - TWO MONTHS LATER

*F*ive p.m. meant rush hour in Sydney. Not just on the roads, but on the footpaths as well. I pushed through the glass doors of my office building and joined the swarm of people bustling toward the parking station where I'd left my car that morning. We were in the thick of autumn, but the evenings were still light and warm, though it wouldn't stay that way for much longer. Soon, I'd be leaving in the dark, with cold wind greeting me. Once those days hit, I'd be cursing these after-work walks and the fact that our building didn't have parking.

My phone buzzed in my bag, "Love Shack" bursting from the tinny speakers. Jamison had personalised his ringtone on my phone a few weeks back, and even though I often got strange looks when he rang me in public, I loved it. It never failed to put a smile on my face.

I swiped the answer button, only to be blasted with a wall of noise. I jerked it away, holding the offending sound at a safer distance from my eardrum. "Jamison?"

The racket in the background settled before Jamison spoke. "Hey babe, sorry about that. It's really loud here. You all done with work? Can you come meet Nathan and me at the games arcade?"

A few weeks back, Jamison had asked if he could pick Nathan up from school on Friday afternoons. Nathan had been all for it when I'd asked him if he'd like that, and it made my life a little bit easier. Jamison was great with him, sometimes taking him down to the soccer fields to kick a ball around, sometimes taking him to kid-friendly places like mini golf. Most weeks I'd come home to them playing Playstation with dinner warm in the oven.

Jamison had made it very clear from the get-go that he wasn't going to try to be Nathan's dad. He already had one. But he wanted to be his friend. And it seemed to be working out pretty well so far, and the two of them were getting along like a house on fire. I could hear Nathan yelling Jamison's name in the background, trying to con him into giving him extra tokens for some game.

"Sounds fun. I'm just walking back to my car, so I'll be thirty minutes or so."

"We'll be here."

"Don't let him play those fighting games though, okay? He's likely to have nightm—"

"Elodie?"

I whipped my head to the side at the sound of my name and the gentle hand on my arm.

"Yes?" I said to the young, brunette woman who'd stopped me as I covered the phone speaker with my hand. There was something familiar about her, and we'd obviously met if she knew my name, but for the life of me, I couldn't place her.

Then it hit me like a sledgehammer.

"Can we talk?"

My eyes widened as I went back to my phone call. "Uh, Jam? I have to go."

"Okay, but which game is it he can't—"

"I…" I said, trying to calm my pulse, which was suddenly out of control. "Bree's here."

"Bree?" Jamison squeaked out, questions about Nathan's video game apparently forgotten. "What is she even doing there? Walk away quickly. Or at least, don't make direct eye contact; she might be there to steal your soul." He chuckled at his own joke.

I ignored him and studied the woman carefully, as she stood waiting for me to finish my call. Her previously long hair had been cut pixie short and dyed a deep brown colour, which looked a thousand times nicer than the brassy blond she'd been sporting the last time I'd seen her. Gone were the towering heels and the top that showed off more cleavage than a stripper. In its place she wore flats with fitted pants and a collared shirt with all but the top button done up. She looked pale without her fake tan, a sprinkling of freckles across her makeup-free face making her seem very young. But the thing that surprised me most was the quiet way she stood, her eyes downturned as she fidgeted with the strap of her bag. I'd never seen her anything but bold and loud. But right now, Bree looked nervous.

I didn't want to cause a scene in the middle of the street. And all my past experiences with Bree said that's exactly how this would end. Jamison was right. I should just walk away from her. I didn't owe her anything. The horrible, hateful words she'd spewed at me that night in the restaurant still played loud and clear in my head. And speaking to her was the last thing I felt like doing right now. Just seeing her burst the happy little bubble Jamison and I had been living in.

But then she lifted her eyes again, and there was an emptiness there that made me freeze. Her expression was that of a woman who'd hit rock bottom and had nothing left. "Please," she said softly.

I bit my lip before breathing out slowly. Then, even to my surprise, I said to Jamison, "It's okay. I can spare a few minutes. See you at the arcade soon."

He was still protesting loudly when I hung up. I tucked my phone back into my bag.

People were being forced to detour around us, but neither of us moved off the crowded footpath. I waited, and the silence drew out, but I wasn't going to be the first to speak. She seemed to be wrestling with herself, but there was obviously something she wanted to say.

"I heard Rick has a new girlfriend..."

I raised an eyebrow, annoyance creeping into my voice. "Is that really why you stopped me? To talk about Rick? Because if so, you're speaking to the wrong person. I'm not up to date on his social life. He's been better about seeing Nathan and not disappointing him since the two of you split, so as long as he keeps that up, I don't care who he chases after." The words came out a bit more snippily than I had planned, but right now, I was missing out on time with Jamison and Nathan. I didn't want to stand here gossiping with Bree about where Rick was sticking his dick. I just didn't care.

"Right. No, of course. I'm sorry. That isn't why I stopped you. This is just..." She pulled her shoulders back before she looked me square in the eye. "I couldn't let you walk past without apologising. I've wanted to for weeks." She looked down at her fingernails but then seemed to find some steel within herself and met my gaze again. "I'm really sorry, Elodie. The things I said to you that night in the restaurant... I'm ashamed of myself." She shifted her bag onto her other shoulder. "Jamison probably told you that I have skeletons in my closet. But I've done a lot of soul-searching since I spoke to him last, and I know I used those things as an excuse. I'm not the only one to have been hurt by someone I loved. But then I went and helped Rick do the same thing to you. I don't deserve or ask for your forgiveness, but I did want you to know that that person who said those horrible things? She isn't me. Not the real me." She shifted her weight from foot to foot. "Not the person I want to be anyway. And I wanted you to know that I'm trying."

I didn't say anything for a long moment, trying, before I opened my mouth, to process all the changes in Bree and her apology. But words escaped me. Never in a million years had I thought I'd ever hear these words from this woman's mouth. She smiled tightly. "Well. That's it. I'll see you around, I guess."

She'd taken a few steps into the crowd before I called her back. "Bree?"

Only the top half of her body turned with her head. "Yes?"

"I'm glad you're trying. I hope you find what makes you whole."

Her bottom lip trembled slightly, her eyes misting. "Thank you. I hope things work out for you too. With Jamison, I mean. He's one of the good ones. Don't let him go."

"I don't plan to." Warmth began to defrost some of my feelings toward her. She was young and broken, and nobody deserved that. She had a lot of years ahead of her, and I truly did hope she could find someone who would treat her well and make her happy. Her posture softened, and she nodded curtly before she turned and disappeared into the crowd.

I finished the walk to my car in record time, not really paying any attention to my surroundings. I didn't need Bree to tell me how lucky I was to have Jamison. I already knew it, with every beat of my heart. Every beat told me I loved him.

Jamison

I couldn't stop staring at the arcade entry. Every time it whooshed open, it caught my eye and I'd hold my breath, waiting to see if it was Elodie. I had a plan. And even Elodie running into Bree wasn't going to stop me from going through with it. It was officially our two-month anniversary, and I'd wanted to say three little words to Elodie for almost the entire time we'd been together. I loved her. There was no doubt in my mind about that. She was beautiful, kind, and we'd fitted into each other's lives seamlessly. Nathan was the coolest kid around, and hanging out with him on Friday afternoons was something I'd looked forward to each week.

I was ready to move things to the next level, but I'd held off on telling her, because I'd wanted to give her time. I wanted her to know I wasn't going to rush this or pressure her into more than she felt ready to give. And I wanted to give Nathan time to fall in love with me too.

But I'd woken up that morning determined I'd waited long enough. The words were on the tip of my tongue, night and day. Even if she didn't feel the same way, I had to tell her today. I had to.

"Ha! I won!" Nathan yelled, drawing my attention back to the video game we'd been playing. The words *you lose* flashed on my side of the screen. I hoped like hell they weren't a metaphor for the rest of the night.

"So you did. Rematch?"

I laser focussed my attention on the next game, determined not to let his little ego get too big. I'd never hear the end of it if he won *every* game.

We were deep in the zombie-killing fields when Elodie appeared between us, one hand slipping around my waist, her other hand ruffling Nathan's hair.

"Hi, Mum! I'm kicking Jamison's butt!" Nathan yelled, his eyes never leaving the screen for a second. But I abandoned the game instantly, dropping my controller, gathering Elodie into my arms and dropping a kiss to her lips. Damn, she was beautiful. Nerves made my stomach lurch as she smiled.

"Well, hi to you too."

I leant back and studied her. "What did Bree want?"

Elodie circled her arms around my back and rested her head

on my chest, squeezing me tight, before she tilted her chin up to look up at me. "She apologised."

I quirked a disbelieving eyebrow. "Did pigs fly?"

She laughed. "And she said I should hold onto you."

I grinned, relieved. "Well, she got that right at least. Not that I plan on letting you go."

Her eyes sparkled. "Good."

For a long moment, we stood there, in a crowded video-game arcade, with Elodie's little boy hollering at the screen and the drone of people and machines around us. But in my mind, we were the only two people in the room. Everything ceased to exist, except for her. The feel of her in my arms, the way my heart thumped against my chest, and the overwhelming feelings churning through me like a punch to the stomach... I couldn't catch my breath. I could stand here forever and still never want to let her go. It was near impossible not to blab my feelings, and it took all my strength to drag my gaze away in order to put my plan into action.

"Hey, Nathan. Now that your mum is here, let's go do photo-booth photos."

He eyed me warily from where he still held his zombie gun controller.

"You can pull silly faces."

"Okay then!" He scampered off to the photo booth, and I linked my fingers with Elodie's as we trailed after him.

"Come on. Let's get in there before someone else does." Nerves and adrenaline made me twitchy.

Nathan pushed aside the grey curtain and disappeared into the booth as Elodie and I caught up. I did the same and stopped short. It was the tiniest photo booth I'd ever seen. There was barely even room for one person on the seat, let alone three.

"You go first, Nate," Elodie said stepping back, but I shook my head.

"No, come on. I want one of the three of us."

Elodie's eyebrows pulled together adorably. "We won't all fit."

"Sure we will. Nathan, jump up. Let me sit first, your mum can sit on my lap, and you can sit on hers."

Elodie looked doubtful, but I sat down and quickly pulled her onto my lap before she could protest.

"Oof," she grunted, as Nathan scrambled up onto her lap, sitting at the top of our human pile like the king of the castle.

"Put some tokens in, kiddo."

Elodie leant forward to help him and I used their momentary distraction to slip two cards from the back pocket of my jeans, keeping them pressed face down on the chair next to me.

All three of us shuffled around, trying to get comfortable in the claustrophobic space, and get our heads within the two red guidelines that showed us where the photo would be cut off. Before we had really worked it out, a robotic sounding voice started up a countdown. 4...3...2..."Silly faces for the first one!" Elodie called.

My heart was beginning to thump wildly, now that my plan was in full swing, and I prayed like mad I'd be able to pull it off and not have her bust me in the middle of it. I stuck my tongue out and crossed my eyes, right before a flash nearly blinded me.

"One more silly one!" Nathan yelled.

4...3...2...

With one hand, I put up bunny ears behind Nathan's head. I used the other to hold up one of the postcard-sized signs I'd drawn in permanent marker that morning, being careful to hold it behind Elodie's line of vision. As soon as the flash lit up the booth, I dropped the card and shoved it behind me.

"A nice one this time," I requested as the machine began to count down for the third time. Nathan groaned, but I hoped he was smiling nicely. This was the important moment. As the countdown hit one, I flashed up my last card, dropping it back to the seat as soon as it was over.

"What are you doing back there?" Elodie asked, twisting back to look over her shoulder.

"Nothing. Quick, kiss me for the last one."

"Happy to oblige," she murmured as her lips brushed mine and the flash went. I pulled her closer instead of letting her move away. Elodie's resistance quickly melted away, her lips parting ever so slightly as she kissed me back.

"Ew!" Nathan yelled, putting an abrupt halt to the moment.

I turned to him and laughed. "I know, right? Tell your mum to quit kissing me all the time!"

Elodie rolled her eyes as Nathan scrambled to get off her lap and pushed the grey curtain aside, opening us up to the view of the entire arcade again. Elodie stood up more slowly and I followed after her. Nathan bounced on the spot outside the booth as he waited for it to spit out our photo strip.

He snatched it from the slot when it appeared, and I watched carefully as he studied it. Then he laughed and looked up at me. "How did you do that?"

"Do what?" Elodie asked as she took the photo strip from Nathan. I winked at him and hugged him to my side with one arm. Then we both turned our attention to where Elodie was looking over the photos. I held my breath. When she looked up, her smile was wide, and her eyes were wet with unshed tears. For a split second, I was super proud of myself for creating such a romantic declaration of love. Until I realised the tears were from laughter.

She clutched her stomach as I looked at her, bewildered. She held the photos out to me, and I groaned when I realised what had happened. The first photo was the three of us pulling ridiculous faces. The second was where I'd flashed up a card that read, *Love you, Nathan*. It was perfect. But the third photo, the one where I'd flashed up a card that read, *And your mum too*, was the source of my instant embarrassment. It was the money shot. But I'd held the card slightly outside of frame. The three lines of text had been cut off. Instead of *And your mum too*, it read *And yo mu to*.

"And yo mu to, huh?" Elodie asked through her laughter. I couldn't help but join in. I should have just gone traditional and taken her out for dinner or something.

"Yeah, I guess so. Damn. I thought that was going to be hella romantic. I wanted it to be perfect for you."

"I think we've already proven that we don't need perfect, don't you?"

In total agreement, I cupped her cheeks in my hands and stared deep into the most beautiful eyes. "I love you, Elodie. You're everything I didn't know I wanted, but everything I need. You and Nathan both."

All traces of humour disappeared from her expression. She blinked, and a tear escaped, rolling down her cheek. My heart swelled, even though I'd thought it already full. Her lip quivered with emotion as she pulled my mouth down to hover above hers. "I love you too," she whispered before I crushed my mouth down onto hers.

For once, Nathan didn't moan about our public display of affection. I felt his little arm around my waist, as both Elodie and I dropped a hand to include him in a group hug.

Who needed perfect when I had all of this?

THE END

You loved to hate her in Only the Perfect, but Bree's story isn't done. Read her scorching new romance in Only the Truth, an Only You bonus story. Now available on Amazon and Kindle Unlimited. Or read on for a sneak peek!

AND GRAB AN EXTRA BONUS BOOK, Only the Lies, for FREE by joining my mailing list here!

ONLY THE TRUTH SNEAK PEEK!

CHAPTER 1

BREE

The second hand on the wall clock ticked on silently, my impatience growing every time it moved. There was a special place in Hell for people who continually ran late. Nothing annoyed me more. Though, I didn't know why I'd expected her to be on time today. She hadn't been on time for any of my other appointments either. "Just go on through to her office, Miss Jacobson. She'll be right with you, Miss Jacobson," I muttered under my breath to the empty therapist's office. Yeah right.

I straightened my pencil skirt, smoothed over my work blouse, and sighed. It wasn't the poor receptionist's fault, and I was being catty. At least I recognised it this time. Closing my eyes, I counted backwards from one hundred, breathing deeply. By the time I got to single digits, the bubbling anger had diminished.

The door behind me finally opened, and a short, dark-haired woman strode into the room, unhurried despite the fact she was over thirty-five minutes late for our five p.m. appointment. She deposited a pile of papers on her desk before sitting primly in her over-sized chair. "Bree. It's been some time."

"Six months."

Dr Guzman scribbled something on a notepad. "So, fill me in." Her gaze tracked carefully over my features, and I straightened my spine, folding my hands neatly in my lap. "How have you been?"

I plastered a smile across my face. "Great. Really great, actually. I have my own apartment now. It's only small, but it's in a great area. I enrolled in a Naturopathy course—"

"Naturopathy? That's…interesting."

I forced myself not to roll my eyes. I still worked my day job, as a makeup artist on a local TV soap, but after the breakdown of my last relationship, I wanted a change. Makeup appealed to my creative side, but I needed something that would exercise other parts of my brain as well. The mentors who ran the course had warned us we'd be given grief for studying alternatives to Western Medicine. They hadn't been wrong. My own mother had scoffed when I'd told her about it during our annual phone call. She'd called it 'hippy rubbish' to be exact. But if I hadn't bothered getting into an argument with her, I certainly wasn't going to try to explain the benefits to this woman.

So, instead, I carried on as if she hadn't spoken. "I've also been doing yoga and meditation and I've taken up cycling. That bike seat is the most contact my vagina has had in that time, too."

Dr Guzman looked up sharply, her pen hovering in midair. "Excuse me?"

My face flushed hot. Oops. Too much information. "I'm still not having sex, is what I meant."

"Right. Right. That's good." She moved to her laptop and scrolled through a file before turning back to me. "You don't have long left on your celibacy vow. Only about a month, according to my records. You've kept it this whole time?"

"Yep."

It had been one of the easier aspects of my therapy. Doctor Guzman had pointed out on our first session that I'd bounced from one toxic relationship to another, ever since I was old enough to realise boys existed. She'd made me write and sign a contract, stating I would avoid relationships or casual sex for a year while I worked through my issues. Not that she could enforce it, of course, but she'd pointed out I needed to make things right within myself before I could take on someone else and their needs. And, at the time, I was so sick of men, it hadn't been difficult to swear them off for a year. Other aspects of my reinvention had been much harder.

"And the anger management course I suggested?"

"Yes," I reported, legitimately pleased to be able to answer in the affirmative. Unlike the last two appointments, where I'd had to answer no because I'd skipped out on going. "I completed it last week. It was great. I really think it's helping. I feel less... highly strung." That was mostly the truth. I did feel less highly strung...when people didn't keep me waiting for forty minutes, anyway.

She raised an eyebrow. "Hmmm..."

I held onto my fake smile, but irritation crept up on me. I hated when she did that. I was here, on time for my appointment. Unlike her. I was talking. Why did she have to *hmmm* me? The woman reminded me of my mother and the disapproval I'd put up with for my entire life. I didn't need this judgement. Not when I was paying her eighty dollars an hour to fix me. The silence drew out between us as she waited, and I studied my shellacked nails, pretending not to know what she was waiting for.

She gave in first. Ha. "And your sister?"

Ugh. There it was. The one thing I hadn't done and the one thing I really didn't want to talk about. "What about her?" We both knew I was stalling, but she played along.

"Did you speak to her, like we discussed last time?"

My fake smile faltered.

"Bree. Don't you think you need to speak to her?"

"No," I stated dully.

She frowned, her eyebrows pulling together in the exact same way my mother's used to.

I really needed a new therapist.

"Fine," I huffed out. "I'll call her." Maybe.

"Today?"

I winced at the thought of making that call. Of speaking to the sister who had been a surrogate mother to me when our own was too busy with her career to care for the children she had never wanted.

The same sister who had then run off and married my high school sweetheart.

We hadn't spoken in years.

I'd let the trauma fester to the point it affected every part of my life, creating a temper I couldn't control. I'd explode into a fiery outburst at the smallest upset. It had almost become my trademark. But after a year of therapy, painstakingly fixing myself, I'd come too far to not finish the process.

"Fine. Today."

IT WAS WELL after six when I finally got out of the therapist's office and unlocked my bike from the stand. Dr Guzman's offices sat amongst several other medical practices and a mixed martial arts gym, with a combined total of three off-road parking spaces. It was impossible to get a spot, so I always cycled.

Normally I enjoyed the ride, as it was only around fifteen minutes from my apartment, but as I pedalled along the side of the building, all I could think of was the late hour. How I should have driven because I had a huge exam tomorrow, and between Dr Guzman being late, and now having to ride home, my study time was slipping away. I'd be pulling an all-nighter at this—

"Fuck!" a deep voice yelled as something huge ploughed into

me at high speed. I careened off the path, wobbling wildly onto the road. Mother of God! What the—

I didn't even get a chance to do any yelling or swearing of my own before my tyre hit a pothole and I crashed headfirst into the unforgiving ground. My helmet cracked as it hit the road, my cheek scraping along the tar in the process. My head spun, but it was my bare shoulder and arm that took the brunt of the fall.

I slid to a stop, my legs tangled around my bike, my skin probably left behind me somewhere judging by the stinging pain in my arm. Damn summer evenings. If it had been winter, I might have had some protection from the road, in the form of a jacket or coat. But this thin blouse had no chance.

At least I was close to medical help, I supposed as I lay there. Though, I blinked at the sky, wondering how helpful a therapist, a dentist, and a gynaecologist would be with probable broken bones and a concussion. I almost laughed. It sounded like the beginning to one of those jokes. Three guys walked into a bar...

As I pondered peeling my aching body off the road, a face appeared above me. A ridiculously handsome face. Dark hair. Hazel eyes. Scruff covering a strong jaw. If I hadn't just been nearly killed, I might have tried slipping him my number.

Why was I even checking him out when I'd just been mowed down? Maybe I really did have a concussion.

"Shit, are you okay?" he asked.

I groaned, my body protesting my attempts at moving. "Something the size of the Titanic just hit me, and now I'm a bloodied mess in the middle of the road. Do I look okay?"

I finally managed to get myself to a sitting position. Frig, my arm really hurt. I glanced down at it and grimaced. Yep, there used to be skin there. "What the hell just happened?"

The guy bent down and lifted my bike off me before he squinted at my wound. "I kind of ran into you. I was coming around the corner, and my phone was ringing, and I was trying to find it in my bag. I didn't even see you. I'm so sorry. Here, let me help you up."

He extended a hand in my direction, but I just stared at it, my brain not comprehending what he was saying. He ran into me? With his car? I gazed past him. No, he'd been on a bike, too. I could see it abandoned on the ground over by where he'd run me off the path. But, he was on his phone? WTF?

I was banged up and now going to be even later for my study session after I went to the ER and got myself fixed up, all because he'd gotten distracted by a phone call? Who was on the other end? The Queen?

The simmering anger I'd been working so hard to keep in check for months now threatened to erupt. Breathe, Bree. Breathe.

But then I saw a badge, dangling from his pocket, *Dr Damien Farrow* printed in neat type beneath a photo of his smiling head. His *stupid*, smiling head! You had to be kidding me. My barely in check rage bubbled over. Fucking doctors!

"You could have killed me, you douche nozzle! Why didn't you just let it go to voicemail? Are you really so important you *had* to take the call that very second?" I went to rub my aching arm, but my fingers came away sticky with blood. My stomach rolled.

"Shit! This is going to need stitches!" My voice came out high and squeaky, and I was probably overreacting, because I had a tendency to do that, but damn it, today was not my day, and I'd had enough. People sucked.

I expected more apologies and maybe some grovelling for forgiveness, but Dr Dickhead's lips curved up and, to my aston-ishment, a chuckle rumbled out of him. "Feisty, aren't you?"

My mouth dropped open. Scratch that about overreacting. The guy probably had awards for asshattery.

"What?" he asked as he took my arm, being careful to keep his fingers away from the blood. "It's a graze. You'll be fine."

"Fine? Easy for you to say. It wasn't your head cracking off the ground! What kind of doctor are you anyway? Don't you have some sort of duty of care to help the people? I could have a concussion for all you know. You didn't even ask me how many fingers you're holding up or anything."

"True." His voice was irritatingly calm in comparison to my yelling. He took my jaw between his fingers, tilting my head. I stilled as his gaze met mine. There were flecks of gold in amongst the hazel, and they were surrounded by long, dark lashes. The skin at the corners crinkled as if he smiled a lot, and there was a twinkle—

A bright light nearly blinded me, causing my eyelids to slam closed. I swatted his hands and doctor's torch out of my face. "What are you doing?"

He threw up his hands in frustration. "Since you implied I was being a shit doctor, I'm checking you for a concussion. How many fingers am I holding up?"

"Oh, for frig sake." I scrambled to stand, pulling my bike up with me. My head felt intact, I was good to go. "I'm fine."

"Your shirt is ripped, and you're bleeding. At least come back to my office. I may just be a gynaecologist, and not much good with concussions, but I can at least fix up a graze for you."

I snorted back a laugh. "You're a gyno?"

He frowned. "I specialise is gynaecology and fertility. Why is that funny?"

"Because you're entirely too young and good-looking to have your head between any woman's legs, unless you're—"

He raised an eyebrow as I realised what I'd said. Shit! I definitely had a concussion. I needed to go to the hospital. "I'm going to go now."

"Have dinner with me tonight?"

I spun back to where he stood with his arms crossed over his chest, one eyebrow raised as if he'd laid down a challenge.

"Why on earth would I do that? You just ran me over with your bike."

He shrugged, an annoying half-smirk, half-grin spreading across his face. "You've got attitude. I like it. And you really may have a concussion so you shouldn't be alone. Plus, you think I'm handsome."

"And arrogant. And possibly blind, considering you didn't even see me riding right in front of you. And anyway. I don't date. So, no thanks. I'll pass." I pushed my bike away, walking it a few steps before I swung my leg over and found the pedals.

"Shame," Dr Knob-Jockey called from behind me. "Because for the record, I'm really good *every* time I have my head between a woman's legs. Not just when I'm at work."

KEEP READING HERE!

ALSO BY ELLE THORPE

The Only You series (complete)

*Only the Positive (Only You, #1) - Reese and Low.

*Only the Perfect (Only You, #2) - Jamison.

*Only the Truth - (Only You, bonus novella) - Bree.

*Only the Lies - (FREE Only You, bonus novella) - Cleo.

*Only the Negatives (Only You, #3) - Gemma.

*Only the Beginning (Only You, #4) - Bianca and Riley.

*Only You boxset

Dirty Cowboy series (complete)

*Talk Dirty, Cowboy (Dirty Cowboy, #1)

*Ride Dirty, Cowboy (Dirty Cowboy, #2)

*Sexy Dirty Cowboy (Dirty Cowboy, #3)

*25 Reasons to Hate Christmas and Cowboys (a Dirty Cowboy bonus novella, set before Talk Dirty, Cowboy but can be read as a standalone, holiday romance)

Buck Cowboys series (Spin off from the Dirty Cowboy series)

*Buck Cowboys (Buck Cowboys, #1)

*Buck You! (Buck Cowboys, #2)

Saint View High series (Reverse Harem, Bully Romance)

*Devious Little Liars (Saint View High, #1)

*Dangerous Little Secrets (Saint View High, #2)

*Twisted Little Truths (Saint View High, #3)

Saint View Prison - (Reverse Harem, Romantic Suspense)

Book 1: Locked Up Liars (Saint View Prison, #1)

Book 2: Solitary Sinners (Saint View Prison, #2)

Book 3: Fatal Felons (Saint View Prison, #3)

Add your email address here to be the first to know when new books are available!

www.ellethorpe.com/newsletter

Join Elle Thorpe's readers group on Facebook!

www.facebook.com/groups/ellethorpesdramallamas

ACKNOWLEDGMENTS

Back when I wrote Only the Positive, I didn't plan to write Jamison a book of his own. I had stories for Gemma (Reese's little sister), Bianca and Riley. But Jamison's story was never part of the plan. I thought he might have been gay for awhile, but then I got to know him better as I wrote Only the Positive, and nope. Not gay. Suddenly the wedding scene was playing out in my head and I HAD to write him a book of his own. Not sometime in the future. But now. I scribbled an outline for his book in about 15 minutes with my hand cramping, then I wrote his story in less than twenty days. I've never had so much fun writing. So thank you to Jamison and Elodie, for being such easy characters to love.

Thank you to Jira and our beautiful kids, Thomas, Felicity and Heidi who let me take two hours each day, even though we were on a camping holiday, to write this book. Thanks for understanding that sometimes the voices in my head won't leave me alone until I let them out :)

Thank you to my writing besties Zoe Ashwood and Jolie Vines. I don't know how I got lucky enough to be adopted by the two of you, but I know I couldn't do it without you. I can't wait to have your books sitting on my shelf!

Thank you to my editor, Erica Russikoff from www.ericaedits.com for correcting my terrible, excessive use of commas, (is that too many commas?) and to Lauren Dawes from www.slyfoxcoverdesigns.com for nailing the cover in pretty much one take.

Huge thank you to my beta team - Michela Hannigan, Kirsty Dyball, Tamara McCall, Shannan Fecht, Sammi Sylvis, Alisa Cavanaugh, Shellie Maddison, Allyson Murphy and Rose White. Your enthusiasm for this book made me so happy, and your critiques were invaluable. You're all amazing. Thank you to all the bloggers, bookstagrammers and authors that helped me promote this book.

And last, but never least, thank you to you guys. The readers. Thank you for investing your hard earned money and time in my stories. I love your messages most of all, so please find me on social media, or my website and drop me a line!

ABOUT THE AUTHOR

Elle Thorpe lives on the sunny east coast of Australia. When she's not writing stories full of kissing, she's a wife and mummy to three tiny humans. She's also official ball thrower to one slobbery dog named Rollo. Yes, she named a female dog after a dirty hot character on Vikings. Don't judge her. Elle is a complete and utter fangirl at heart, obsessing over The Walking Dead and Outlander to an unhealthy degree. But she wouldn't change a thing.

You can find her on Facebook and Instagram (@ellethorpe-books or hit the links below!) or at her website www.ellethorpe.com

f facebook.com/ellethorpebooks
o instagram.com/ellethorpebooks
g goodreads.com/ellethorpe
p pinterest.com/ellethorpebooks